CONQUEST

HAROLD GODWINSON

The Last Saxon King

Barry Upton

. . . about Harald Hardrada, The Last Viking

the first in the Conquest series -

"An exciting read" ****

With a surface-level knowledge of the Battle of Hastings and having seen the Bayeux Tapestry, I delved into Barry's book with a lot of curiosity about the untold, and partly imagined, past of Harald Hardrada (a man I only knew of from his famous 'final image'). This book is an immensely enjoyable speculation into his formative years, and it is always refreshing to read a protagonist that isn't instantly likeable! Despite his flaws, you are drawn into Harald's tale and must see it through to its inevitable conclusion. An exciting read for those who are intrigued by our ancient past.

(Debora E Wilson, author of "The Artist's Muse")

HAROLD GODWINSON - THE LAST SAXON

Conquest is the first series of historical fiction written by Barry Upton.
Details of the earlier novels, plays and musicals can be found on the website: https://barryuptonauthor.com or by scanning QR code below

What readers have said about earlier books:

A really enjoyable read…

The characters are clearly and realistically defined…

Astute understanding of the trauma of adolescence.

Thoroughly enjoyed reading this book…

Sometimes disturbing and sometimes sad but a gripping, well written book right from the start…

Hard to put down!

Please add your review on the Amazon site.

HAROLD GODWINSON - THE LAST SAXON

CONQUEST...

... is a trilogy of Historical Novels, centred around the momentous and tumultuous year of 1066; three titles each focusing on a key figure in the story of the Conquest of England. They are not sequential, but tell three parallel stories of the key players, men and women, of the year 1066.

The first book, published in December 2022, starts in Norway where **Harald Sigurdsson**, already King of Norway, sets his eyes on conquest. This is Harold Hardrada who became known as "the last Viking".

This book, the second, published in December 2023, looks at the rise of **Harold Godwinson**, later Harold II, "the last Saxon", and his rise to power before his defeat at Hastings.

The third focuses on **William Duke of Normandy**, "the Bastard", who feels he has a legitimate right to become King of England.

 These three novels in the Conquest series tell the story of the most significant year in English, perhaps even European history, through the eyes of its three principal protagonists.

HAROLD GODWINSON - THE LAST SAXON

It is not my role, as a novelist of historical fiction, to change facts, only to invent fictions. Much of what is recorded here can be verified by reading the **Anglo-Saxon Chronicles.** Little is known of his early life, which gave me scope to explore how Harold Godwinson's character was moulded and shaped to become the ambitious man known as "the last Saxon". He was determined that England would be a truly Anglo-Saxon country, drawing on the past heroes back to *Alfred The Great*, and saw himself to be the means that this could be achieved.

I have frequently used place names that would have been familiar to eleventh century people, rather than their modern-day equivalents. While the story is rooted in the chronicles, it is *my invention,* and I make no apology for this being a work of fiction.

I hope there is enough fact to be of interest to scholars of the eleventh century, and enough fiction to delight those who enjoy a good story.

This story is told in several voices, all characters who were close to Harold Godwinson; all characters who could paint a picture of the boy, the man and the king. Their stories are as accurate as the author can make them, and serve to give an holistic view of the central figure.

HAROLD GODWINSON - THE LAST SAXON

HAROLD:

I know what they say of me. All of them, even my own family. That I am self-seeking. That I am ruthless. That I will stop at nothing to get my desires. But their "ruthless" is my "determined". I have a solemn duty to ensure that this land of ours, this England, remains a Saxon land; that it will never again be subject to the whims and taxes of a foreign king. We have had our share of Viking warlords. I will fight them with the last drop of my blood. We have had enough of their heathen ways.

And now there is talk of a Norman invasion, as if England deserved no better than a bastard Duke. And all because of a promise made by a weak king in a moment of brain-fever. No! It is time that England became what it truly is - a Saxon Kingdom. And who better to bring it about, than a Saxon Earl; and am I not the best, the most noble and the bravest of them all?

Let them say what they wish to say. Let them call me ruthless and self-seeking, but I am Harold, son of Godwin and I am destined to become King of England.

Tostig

HAROLD GODWINSON - THE LAST SAXON

TIDES

- What makes the sea move?

It was a reasonable question from a young boy who grew up in the rolling hills. My brothers laughed at the question. Harold wasn't even the oldest of us! That was Sweyn. But that never stopped him from acting as though it were he and not Sweyn who was the most senior. He was seven years old when I was born and my earliest memories of him are of a sometimes kindly, but more often teasing older brother. I saw little of Sweyn who seemed to spend much of his time in the company of local monks, memorising great chunks of the bible, even learning the skills of illustrated writing, a skill more usually associated with the women in our family. But Sweyn said he was dedicated to the work of God. By the time I was old enough to explore the estates, learning to shoot an arrow, to kill a wild boar, to bring down a deer, Harold was already at the court of King Cnut. Three of us, brothers by birth but not by inclination, all led separate lives: the church, the court and the estate. There were times however when all three of us were together.

I was still very young, five or six, I think, but I remember a visit to the wide-open stony beach a few miles south of our home at Senlac.

- It is never still. It is like a strange and restless animal.

Sweyn made no reply. He was alongside the King who had invited his loyal earls and his younger son to join the royal party. It was Harold, selecting stones to hurl into the water, watching them bounce on the surface, who spoke.

- What a dolt you are, Tostig. The sea is not an animal.

I had him there. Of course, it was an animal. Look how it moved, how it roared.

HAROLD GODWINSON - THE LAST SAXON

- *It is you who are the dolt, big brother. What can it be if not an animal? See how it moves; listen to the roars; feel its power.*

But Harold wandered further down the beach looking for thinner and smoother stones. I could hear his laughter coming back up the beach. I reddened at his mockery. I felt my mother's hand take mine and pull me back away from the water. And she shouted across to Harold.

- *Tostig is no different from how you were at his age, Harold. Give him time to grow, to understand.*

But Harold was out of earshot or pretended to be. She brought me back up the beach and replaced my boots which I had removed earlier to keep them from the waves. The king sat on a giant chair out of reach of the water.

- *The king has asked us to join him, all of us. He has a lesson for us.*

King Cnut was a mighty man – or so he seemed to my childhood self. When he was standing, he was head and shoulders above other men, and his strength was well chronicled. His thick woolly beard and the crown perched above his brow made him twice as imposing and I always felt afraid in his company. Father, Harold and Sweyn stood alongside him, among the other earls and their sons. I wanted to tell them to move further back, for the sea creature was getting ever closer. I pulled at mother's hand.

- *Can the king not see what is happening? The sea is getting closer and soon it will bite his toes.*

This brought laughter from everyone, none louder than Harold, and I felt the colour rise again in my cheeks.

- *Be gentler with the boy.*

It was Cnut who had spoken. I looked up at him and he beckoned me towards him. Father had often spoken of the king; of how he was not an old man, but he would not live much longer. He had travelled far and wide across the seas, even to the coronation of Conrad, the Holy Roman Emperor, to whom we said prayers every day. All this travel, father had said, had weakened him, put a strain on his heart. Soon the kingdoms would pass to Harthacnut, his eldest son who was in Norway attending to the rebels there. Father had said that Harthacnut would make a good king, a strong brave soldier, unlike the king's younger son Harold. *He has a reputation for running away.* I didn't think running away was such a bad thing so long as he was a fast-footed runner.

- *I am a king, Tostig, but I recognise the wisdom in your words. This sea, this water creature has so much power.*

- *But you are a mighty king. You have more power than anyone in this land, more power even than this creature.*

- *See how wise the boy is. He recognises the power and greatness of his king. I used this creature of his, rode on his back to this very spot where we stand. I led an army of Vikings, two hundred ships and one thousand men, and became King of England. And all on the back of this wild sea creature.*

- *If you ordered him to retreat, he would be too afraid to bite your toes! You are king not just of England, but of Denmark and Norway too.*

- *And once of Scotland, but that is another story, eh, boy?*

From Harold, I had heard the stories of Scotland. The wild men from the north had raided again and again far to the north, and Prince Harold had led the English soldiers with little success. Eventually the king had given up the claim he had.

- *Who can resist you, mighty king? Who can stand against you?*

HAROLD GODWINSON - THE LAST SAXON

There was more laughter, until Cnut silenced it by raising his hand high. The waves were creeping closer, and I looked at the King's soft leather boots. They would be ruined unless he ordered the sea to halt. Slowly, sedately, majestically King Cnut stood. He was a tall man, but his shoulders were a little bent, and his eyes showed something of the strain it must be to be a king. He turned his back to the water and looked instead at the sea of faces

- *The boy has guessed my purpose. What wisdom comes from your boy, Godwin.*

There was no laughter now. And I felt proud. Especially when the king told my father that I was wise.

- *I have come to show you how powerful is your king. All of you stand behind me, a little way. All except young Tostig.*

He turned back to the water, stretched his hand out to me and I took it. I know he must have felt me shaking, but he held it in his strong grip, and gradually I relaxed. And all the time the sea climbed closer. He saw my eyes looking first at the sea, and then at my new boots.

- *What is it, boy? Are you afraid that the king cannot halt this tide? Are you afraid for your boots?*

Then he dropped my hand and held both of his arms outstretched, towards the encroaching tide.

- *You are subject to me, as the land on which I am sitting is mine, and no one has resisted my right to its lordship with impunity. I command you, therefore, not to rise on to my land, nor to presume to wet the clothing or limbs of your master.*

I clapped my hands in delight. Now we shall see the power of King Cnut. This creature will have to turn back. But the sea kept rising and drenched the king's feet as well as my own. Soon it was up to his shins, and I felt the water through the knees of my breeches. He took my hand again and together we walked backwards until we were out of reach. I was dumbstruck. I could say nothing. And in that I was not alone. No-one spoke. This creature had advanced against the king without any retribution, showing no fear of his majesty. Eventually we were on dry stones again, and the king returned to his throne which had been carried back onto drier ground. The king stayed standing, turned to his prince and his earls and called out above the crashing sound of the sea behind him.

- *Let all the world know that the power of kings is empty and worthless, and there is no king worthy of the name save Him by whose will heaven, earth and the sea obey eternal laws.*

And it was Sweyn who shouted the first *Amen*.

As the son of an earl, whose family was kin to the king himself, I grew up in the midst of intrigue. Harthacnut had not returned. It was Harold who explained it all to me.

- *And what is a regent?*
- *It is someone who rules in the king's place?*
- *And Harold is the regent?*
- *Yes.*
- *Then who is the king?*
- *Harthacnut. He is the eldest son of the late king, so he will inherit the title.*
- *But if he is not here…*
- *That is why Harold sits on the throne. Until Harthacnut returns from Norway.*

HAROLD GODWINSON - THE LAST SAXON

- And if he doesn't return?

- That is a good question, Tostig. For a young boy!

I had heard my father and brothers talk together. When Cnut died, they had all assumed that the chosen heir, Harthacnut, would become king in his place. But he was still in Norway, fighting Cnut's enemies. They thought that Harold "Harefoot" was a poor substitute for his brother but because he was next in line there was nothing else for it. I heard what they said, and remembered it, but at the time it seemed confusing. Father took me on his knee and tried to make it clear, but he was too impatient for my questions, so it was left to brother Harold.

- We are Saxons, descended from a long line of noble families, and now our family sits amongst the highest in England. We are loyal to our king, of course we are, for they give us the power. But we want this country of ours to return again to its Saxon roots, and we are the family to do it, when the time comes.

- But kings are born to rule, is that not so?

- It is, little brother, but it doesn't have to be. It would be better if the wise men of our country, The Witan, took the decision for themselves, so that we are not left with an absent king and a weak regent in his place.

I understood the words, but their meaning was not at all clear then.

There were regular meetings of Wessex earls. They came to our house in Senlac and talked long into the night, long after I was in bed, but the mornings were often full of the discussions that had been held, and I picked up morsels, like crumbs left on the table. Harefoot had been made king, after two years of waiting for his brother to return. But it seems that the same seas that had brought his father to power had brought his step-brothers to fight against him. My father

HAROLD GODWINSON - THE LAST SAXON

had stood by the king – however unsuitable he was – and in a fierce battle, the rebels were beaten back into the sea and those that survived fled across it, back to Norway. Alfred, one of the king's stepbrothers was captured by my father, and he was brought to Ely where he begged mercy from the king. Blinded and dying of his wounds, Alfred's body was thrown into a ditch, as a clear lesson to others who might try to seize power. Edward, the dead prince's brother had escaped and sailed to join his mother, Queen Emma at Antwerp where he would be sheltered. It was not uncommon for the king to summon my father to court at Westminster. I remember one such time, when Harold and I accompanied him.

- So, Godwin. It is you I must thank that I still sit safe on my throne and English men and women rest easy in their beds.

- We earls of Wessex have always been loyal to our king.

- And in return you have profited much. You have risen to be among the greatest in the land.

- We are loyal, and we receive the king's gifts as reward for our constant, unwavering support.

- Then I have a task for you. I will follow my father sooner than I had hoped. I have had a premonition of my own death, and I want to be sure England remains with my father's blood. There are many abroad who will seek to take the kingdom from us. King Magnus of Norway, or Edward, son of Edmund Ironsides, with the support of Harald Sigurdsson. And others across the sea lick their lips at the thought of an empty throne. Find my brother. Tell him England needs him at home. He must take his rightful place as king when I am dead.

Later, in the bedroom I shared with my older brother, I wanted to know more.

- I thought father didn't like this king.

HAROLD GODWINSON - THE LAST SAXON

- It is not about liking or not liking, Tostig. You will come to understand this. We must retain our place in the world, keep our power in England. And most importantly, keep the Northern invaders away. Our father is Kingmaker. It is in his hands.

I was beginning to understand how things worked. I was, after all, nearly ten now, and I was learning fast. Harold Harefoot was only king because my father and others like him had supported his claim. *Better a fool in England than a warrior abroad,* is what my father had said.

My brother sailed for Norway. He was going to meet Harthacnut; his mission was to bring the true king back to England.

HAROLD GODWINSON - THE LAST SAXON

TOUGH-KNOT

I knew Harthacnut by reputation – and by his hair. I had seen him at my father's house many times. As a young timid boy, I had watched him practise sword-fighting in the courtyards, and later, when Harold was in his early teenage years, they would spar together. This future king fought fiercely, and always his hair was tied back and knotted on the top of his head. That is where the name "tough-knot" originated. In quiet corners, there was some disquiet over his rise to become heir. It seems old King Cnut had spurned the children of his first queen and given precedence to their stepbrothers. My father talked with me over the breakfast meal. My father, like the other Saxon earls, wanted a Saxon King for a Saxon country. Tough-Knot was a Viking, who seemed to care more for the Northern Kingdoms than for affairs in England. Ethelred had started the move to wipe Danelaw from England, but it had only limited success. Cnut had taken his revenge and now we were annexed firmly to the cold countries of the north-east. All this was part of my education.

- *But for the wars in Denmark, Tough-Knot would be king. He seems to care little for England. He should have been here instead of his cowardly brother. But Harefoot is dying. It is time to return the kingdom to Cnut's heir. Your brother will bring him home. Let us hope he is in time. If Harefoot dies before Tough-Knot arrives there will be other Vikings on our doorstep, battling for power.*

Then father was gone, before I had any chance to ask the questions that turned in my head. Harold was due home in the next day or so. His ship had been seen at Orkney. It was the Godwins – our family – who would welcome him; it was the Godwins who would be at his side when he was seated in the great Abbey at Winchester; it was the

HAROLD GODWINSON - THE LAST SAXON

Godwins who would be ready, waiting should the tide turn. The breakfast table was being cleared, and mother was directing the servant girls to their day's chores. I grabbed at her sleeve, and she smiled at me.

- *How you have grown, Tostig. See your head is already up to my shoulder.*

- *What is he like, this Harthacnut? What sort of king will he be?*

- *One with good counsellors, you can be sure, Tostig.*

- *You mean father.*

- *Yes. But not him alone. The Witan will stand with him and guide him wisely. They will not let him betray us as he did his father.*

- *What did he do?*

- *He was a boy, then, and easily swayed, but Cnut forgave him and where the old king led, we shall follow. Unless of course...*

She stopped to berate one of the girls who had dropped a whole jug of water onto the rush floor and left me hanging.

- *Unless... mother?*

- *He will not be allowed to make another such mistake. Not here. Not in England. He has forsaken his duties to us once. Never again!*

Then she was gone, and the room was empty but for me, sitting, lost in my thoughts.

It was a hot day, just two weeks before the mid-summer celebrations. The clothes I had been squeezed into were rough and warm. But mother had insisted that I should look like the son of an earl. Tough-knot's mother was back in England. A ship had brought her from Brugensis, and she was there on the harbour wall at Sandwic, watching as Harthacnut's ship docked. I stood at my mother's side, a little way back from my father and the other earls. I could see him talking with Queen Emma. Even from where I stood, I could see the tension that stood between them, like a wall. I looked at my mother and saw that she had seen the same.

- *She blames your father for her son Alfred's death. And Harefoot too, of course. She will not rest until she has vengeance.*

Father's voice was raised. He was angry and I could see his fists clenched.

- *You cannot think that it is a good idea. Two sons, both at the same time. And why so many ships? Over sixty warships? Does your son think we are here to oppose him? Didn't I send my own son, Harold to bring him back?*

I crept nearer to the front and heard the steel in the queen's reply.

- *You Godwins are not to be trusted. Was it not your hand that slew my son Alfred and threw his body into a ditch?*
- *I acted for the king, madam.*
- *You acted for yourself. The king commanded no respect among you Saxon earls. I hear it was your earls who killed Harefoot.*
- *Harefoot did not die by a Saxon hand. And it was you who sent a rebel army with your two sons at its head. And now your answer is to bring both your sons to England?*
- *Edward will keep his brother safe.*
- *And why should Harthacnut not feel safe here in his kingdom?*
- *We know what you Saxon earls think of us. We know that you will drive us out one day and put your own sons upon the throne. Harold perhaps or even young Tostig.* My ears burned. Me? King? Is that what she meant?

HAROLD GODWINSON - THE LAST SAXON

- He comes prepared. With an invasion force.

- Which, madam, I have no doubt, England will pay for. Has he learned nothing from his days in Denmark? The people hate to pay taxes. Especially to a Viking King. And he may pay for it sooner than he thinks!

Whatever riposte she had prepared, there was no time for it to land. Tough-Knot had stepped down on to English sand. He took a handful and let it fall gently to the ground in a constant flow.

- See how I take possession of this land. Harold Harefoot has held it in my absence. And now I am returned. And we shall hold him accountable for my brother's death.

- And you, Godwin, Emma hissed beside my father.

Alongside Harthacnut stood Harold, my brother. He held Tough-Knot's hand high, like he was heralding a victory.

- See how our conquering hero comes to take back England. And England welcomes him.

Cheers went up from the crowd assembled there on the beach. But they sounded hollow, even to my young ears.

From Sandwic we returned home, hosting the new king at Senlac. And after just a few days' rest, Tough-Knot, with his earls beside him, travelled north to London. My father insisted that all the Godwins be present. I had never seen a coronation before, so I was excited to be going.

- So, little brother. What do you make of it all?

- I make of it, that father is still angry, Harold.

- Tough-Knot goes out of his way to make our father angry, Tostig.

- Is it true that he had Harefoot's body taken out of his grave? His own brother's body?

- *Half-brother, Tostig. It was done at his mother's insistence. And they threw the dead king's body in the Thames, but not before he had the head separated from the body.*
- *I heard that some of the Thames watermen found it and had it buried again.*
- *I heard the same, but we cannot know the truth of it.*

Then, when the king's soldiers came, we all assumed it was an escort to accompany us to the coronation. But they took father away in chains. At first we feared we would never see him again, but Harold and I were told to follow. We were to be present at the trial.

The story of the death of King Edward the Martyr was well known to us. And Corfe Castle was still supposed to be haunted by the king's soul. It happened over fifty years ago now, but the story lives still, even though few people from those days were still alive. The story told of how the murdered king's stepmother was to blame. Queen Aelfthryth was a witch who had cast a spell on him. There were many who believed that the king's mother, Queen Emma was similarly powered; and when Tough-Knot took the throne, it was no surprise that she sat alongside him. We were more afraid of her than we were of him.

He had shown mercy to my father; witnesses were found to swear that he had reluctantly acted on the orders of Harold Harefoot. Their testimony - and the gift of a richly decorated ship, which no Viking can refuse – saved him, but it was clear there was no love lost between the royal family and our own. We settled back to life at

HAROLD GODWINSON - THE LAST SAXON

Senlac; my brother and father banned from the court. My father would hold clandestine meetings with other earls. He was certain that spies told the king, but the meetings were never interrupted. My father was an outspoken critic.

- *The king is over-reaching himself. We English have become used to a way of government that allows wise men's council to prevail. This Danish king has brought his Danish ways with him. The Vikings are autocrats, preferring fear to persuasion and argument. He thinks he can intimidate us.*

Eadwulf, the mighty earl from Northumbria spoke up next.

- *We may seem cowed and fawning, Godwin, but we lie in wait for the day we can safely remove him. We must be rid of this king. But we must act with caution. While the witch lives...*

- *The fleet has doubled in size. Who is this king protecting himself from? From his own people. And with good cause. They get restless and will not stand for this much more.*

And so it went on. Long into the night, long after I'd been sent to my bed. When I emerged for breakfast, the earls had gone.

News came in the morning. Eadwulf had been ambushed on his way back north. He, and his men had been butchered on the roadside, despite the king giving him promises of safe travel. The hall was empty except for my mother and younger siblings.

- *They have gone to London, your father and brother, Harold. The king has commanded them to attend the wedding of Tovi, the king's standard-bearer. We are to follow on. Now go to your rooms. The servants will help you get ready. We are to travel to London before noon.*

We were all excited. To be summoned by the king – even by this king – was a wonderful thing for a boy of my age.

HAROLD GODWINSON - THE LAST SAXON

The king's goblet fell to the floor with a crash, metal on stone. I watched him as he lay writhing in agony. The earls stood in disbelief. All eyes were drawn to Queen Emma. She watched as Harthacnut writhed in agony, then calmly she picked up the crown that lay where it had rolled from Harthacnut's head and placed it on her Edward's head. The half-brother had succeeded. And so, in such a way, England had a new king. Another Viking.

The King's death was a shock to me. It was later, much later, when we had all returned to Senlac that Harold and I spoke of it. Harold had spent time with the king and knew him well:

- *He was a drunkard. He died as he lived, with a surfeit of wine.*

- *Some say it was witchcraft.*

- *Well, if it was, then we need look no further than the tyrant's mother.*

I looked at my brother, who could scarcely hide the smile that played on his lips. There was something he knew that he wasn't saying, at least not to me.

- *Others talk of poison.*

- *My little brother listens to too much gossip. Father and I will attend the coronation. Another Viking king is to be crowned, to rule over Saxon people. But I have more hopes for this one. Edward is more pious than his brother. And he listens to us, understands us. Perhaps this time, England will have the king it deserves.*

- *Is he not a Viking like his half-brother?*

- *He is, little brother. But this one is different.*

HAROLD GODWINSON - THE LAST SAXON

- How?

- He understands how England works. He has promised to restore the royal house of Wessex. What is more, he will marry your sister, Edith. Our family will sit at the heart of the court. Where we belong.

When he had gone, I was left wondering which of the rumours, if any, was true. Witchcraft? Poison? My brother had spent much time with the king; he had been a constant companion. Our father had urged him to be so. And yet I knew they both hated him. And now the king was dead. Top-Knot was gone. In his place we have Edward. And the house of Wessex was to be restored. Whether the rumours were true or not, the Earl of Wessex, my father, and his heirs, had certainly profited. They would have a place close to the throne. They would have a place close to his ear. They would have power.

HAROLD GODWINSON - THE LAST SAXON

WALES

My eldest brother was Sweyn. Throughout much of my youth, I saw little of him. Mother had never forgiven him for dragging our name through the dirt. He had claimed that he was the illegitimate son of Cnut, from a liaison between my mother and the old king. The one thing you learn very quickly when you live amongst great families is that rumour and gossip abound. The story about my brother's parentage had been suppressed. My mother swore under oath that Sweyn was the son of Godwin, just as the rest of us were, but it still rumbled along in the background, and every so often it would emerge. When he reappeared at Senlac, the rumours surfaced again. There was good reason to doubt that he was my true brother. In so many ways he resembled the old king; there was the look of the Viking about him. Our mother was herself descended from a line of Danish nobles and said he resembled her brothers and uncles. But the stories wouldn't go away. I think that was why he spent so little time with the rest of us. If it were true, then he was a threat to the king himself! I liked my eldest brother. He would take time from his studies and visit us, and I was made to feel special in his company. I think he was my mother's favourite, her first-born son. He often brought with him, to show me, the illustrated manuscripts he had produced, many of them prayers and psalms, which he taught me.

- *There is much to be done, Tostig…* He always called me by my name and not "little brother" that Harold always used… *much to be done. This country of ours still has many unbelievers, people who worship pagan gods, especially amongst our northern Viking cousins.*

- *I thought that since Cnut had followed the Cross, the old gods had been laid to rest.*

HAROLD GODWINSON - THE LAST SAXON

- Nothing is so simple, Tostig. Peasants pray to any god that can offer help. If Christ doesn't change their fortunes, they turn to other deities - false gods - to deliver better harvests or fatter cows.

I thought about what Sweyn had said. I suppose it made sense. I, myself, had often had cause to doubt that God had heard my prayers, and wondered whether there was a better way to get what I wanted. As my father's eldest son - despite the rumours! - Sweyn became an earl when I was still only thirteen. Watching him receive this title from the king at Westminster, at the king's court, I felt proud of him, and a little jealous. I couldn't wait to grow up so that I could have my own titles and land. Even Harold, now a strong willowy man of twenty years, was being prepared to become Earl of East Anglia. Sweyn was to take charge of the lands bordering the Welsh. I had never seen a Welsh man or woman, but I knew from all that Sweyn had told me they were wild and rebellious, and wanted to take land away from King Edward, whose rule of those border places was challenged. There were regular reports of skirmishes, so Sweyn was to be sent to quash them, and to establish the borders, by force if negotiations would not work. Wales was a long way from us in Senlac - several days' ride through inhospitable country. I couldn't help thinking that this was another ruse to keep Sweyn out of the way. He looked grand in his furs and chains, but with me he was just a big brother.

- So, Tostig. Your big brother is off to bring these rebels to heel. I have spent long enough in the company of monks. Now is the time for me to show I am a warrior. Just like my father.

I resisted the urge to ask which father he meant.

- Take care of your sisters and prepare yourself for your future role. You are an earl in waiting and still have much to learn.

HAROLD GODWINSON - THE LAST SAXON

- *So, little brother, now that you are almost a man, you must prepare yourself for what is to come.*
Harold was making a rare visit from London.
- *And what is to come, Harold?*
- *Our father grows older, and he will need help to be sure the Godwin name stays strong - and feared. There are many earls who would take our place if they could. There are even some who seek to overthrow the King himself.*
- *But not us, Harold, even though he is a Viking king?*
I noted the smile that played around my brother's mouth.
- *We must show our loyalty until our time comes. And then we shall show our mettle.*
- *I'm not sure I understand, Harold.*
- *These things are too complex for you to grasp, little brother. But you will come to understand.*
- *Understand what?* I was tired of Harold's patronising tones. *What is there to understand?*
- *We are Saxon Earls. Your grandfather was Wulfnoth, Thane of Sussex. But he was stripped of his rank, his titles and his land because jealous thegns spread rumours that he was disloyal to King Ethelred.*
I recalled the story. It had cast a stain on us for many years. My grandfather was falsely accused of stealing the king's ships and he fled with a number of the ships that were loyal to him. There were accusations that he had ransacked coastal towns in the south.

- All this was the work of rivals. He was no traitor. But under the new king, Cnut, our father redeemed our family name. He supported Cnut against the weak boy king Edmund, and once Cnut took the throne, our father was rewarded. Titles were restored and Godwin's name has become synonymous with loyalty. Our mother's Danish heritage has also stood us in good stead. And we, Godwin's sons, are to benefit from our father's wisdom and courage. And under this new king, we shall flourish. And we shall become powerful.

It was clear now. I understood.

- While the King holds us in esteem, we support him.

There was Harold's smile again.

- So, little brother, you begin to see how this works.

And I did. This was not about loyalty. It had never been about loyalty. It was about advantage.

- And how must I prepare?

- You will be head of the household once I am gone. You must look after our mother and sisters. While the men are away, you, little brother, must grow up quickly. We must always be watchful, for there are still many among us who would take our power away again.

So. Tostig, the "little brother", would be in charge of the household. It was time to grow up.

News of Sweyn got back to us. Letters came addressed to my father at Senlac and in his absence, I opened them and relayed his news to my family. Copies had gone to the king, I knew, and so Harold and my father would have heard before us.

At first, Sweyn wrote, *I planned to seek a peaceful resolution. The Welsh people have their own ways, many of them strange to us, but we worship the same God, and they seem reasonable men. Griffith is their leader here in the north. He has driven out the pagans and established himself a strong military base. He has sworn an oath of peace, and he will hold to his borders. The dyke of the great Mercian king, Offa, will once again be observed as the legal borders of our territories. He has pulled back from those settlements that had been claimed that are on the English side of the border. We have peace. And we have Christian folk on our borders. However, there is a price to be paid.*

I peered over the letter from Sweyn and looked into the faces of my mother and siblings and spoke with as much confidence and authority as I could muster - more than I felt, certainly.

- There is always a price to be paid for peace, is that not so, mother?

Mother nodded and smiled. I returned to Sweyn's letter.

I have crossed into Wales with an army to support Griffith in his attempt to quell the troops of the rebellious king of Deheubarth. His name is also Griffith, which causes us much confusion!

There were laughs from my sisters, and I could imagine Sweyn's smile behind the words.

The battle is almost won. I shall return home soon. I shall travel via Leominster, a grand town on the river just over the border which has a fine abbey whose history, though not as ancient as our own abbey, is certainly as revered. There is a woman there...

Mother took the letter from me. I think she feared what may lie in the final paragraph of the letter.

- See, children, your big brother has forgotten nothing of his days as a Christian scholar.

It was the next day that Harold returned to Senlac. It seems that Sweyn had abducted the abbess of Leominster, in an attempt to marry her and, in doing so, gain control of the vast estates she controlled. The king was furious with him. As was Harold.

- Has he learned nothing of our history? His rashness threatens to undo all the good work done by our father. We shall be cast out again. Our father stays with the king, trying to persuade him that it is a rash and foolish act by a rash and foolish man. The king has made it clear that only Sweyn's banishment can save us.

My mother clutched her hand to her breast.

- Where will he go?

- He has fled to Flanders. He seeks refuge with Count Baldwin.

This was such a shock to me. Sweyn had gone. Would he ever return? I asked Harold:

- Will the king be satisfied? Will he ever be able to return home?

- He will not be able to return home any time soon. As for the king, he would rather the Godwins were kept close to him. For now. But take heed, little brother. We walk a narrow path. It is a simple thing to slip off it into murky waters.

It was our mother who had the last word.

- Your sister will keep us safe. She is our saviour as surely as Christ. Edith is Queen and she will look after the Godwins. Meanwhile Sweyn will be safe with Baldwin in Flanders.

The peace with Wales seemed secure and Sweyn's titles and land were forfeit to the king. In his place, Harold became my father's heir. I missed Sweyn. I missed his kindness, his wisdom, his optimism. But Sweyn's name was forbidden to be spoken. And I was now the second son. I was growing into the role too. New outfits, more fit for a nobleman, rather than his son, were made and I spent more of my time at Edward's court. I thought often of Sweyn, and then suddenly an opportunity came to visit him. I was aware that the time had come for a betrothal to be announced. Even I understood that marriages were matters of convenience, of pacts, of politics. And my mother announced that I was to be married to Judith, the old Count Baldwin's daughter; the new one's half-sister. Flanders would become a powerful ally with such a marriage - an ally of the king as well as the Godwins who served him. Judith was the only child of the Count by his second wife, Eleanor of Normandy, and so the peace network grew. Flanders and Normandy were already brought together; now they would become allies of England through marriage to one of the most important families of the land. I had seen a portrait of the girl - she was three years younger than me, and I thought of her as still a girl even though she was the same age as Gunhild, who had grown in the last years to become a young woman. I had watched her development with curious eyes: her growing breasts fascinated me. Harold was to accompany me to Flanders in advance of my mother and father. He wanted to meet Sweyn, in secret. Mother had packed our bags and we rode southward to the coast where a boat lay waiting for us. We arrived at Hastings late in the day. There were rooms reserved for us and after we had seen our bags safely stored, Harold led me down to the port where candles burned so bright it was almost like daytime. Young women flocked around the sailors who had recently docked there and whose purses bulged. They would stay the night at the local inn before setting off for home to wives and families. Two of these young women attached themselves to us. I felt my cheeks burn as one of them threw her arms around me and led me off to her room overlooking the inn yard. Harold had disappeared, presumably with his own woman attached.

HAROLD GODWINSON - THE LAST SAXON

- Your brother tells me you are to be married.

- You know my brother?

- Harold Godwinson is no stranger to this place.

I took her meaning. It bothered me that Harold should be a regular visitor to the beds of these women. It was well known that Harold had taken a bride in "the Danish way", not blessed by the church. Edith was a regular visitor to Senlac, and despite the informal nature of the marriage she was made welcome by my mother. This same brother, it seemed, was well known among the bawds who ran the houses in Hastings.

- Your brother wanted me to prepare you for marriage, young Tostig.

In the shadows of the street, the woman had seemed young but here by the light of the candle which she lit, I saw that she was older, perhaps several years older than me. Together we went to my room, and once there she guided me onto the bed where I sat and watched as she undid the cords that fastened her tunic. There was nothing underneath, none of the frilled lace underclothes that I occasionally saw on my sister. Her breasts were large, and I sat in silence feeling the movement between my legs. When she was naked, she moved towards me and undressed me.

In the morning she was gone, but the stale smell of her lingered in the room and on my body. I poured cold water over my body and dried myself vigorously then dressed quickly. Did this one night prepare me for marriage? Was it as simple and straightforward as that? Or would my new wife be very different? Harold had appeared in my room with a wide grin on his face. Together we descended to the breakfast table, which was laid out for us.

- Are you ready, little brother?

- Ready?

HAROLD GODWINSON - THE LAST SAXON

- For what is to come?

- I hope so, Harold.

- It was our father who brought me here, when I was your age.

- And were you then ready for Edith?

- Nothing could have prepared me for Edith. She has a grace that surpasses all other women.

- But you knew…

- I knew how to enjoy her, little brother.

- Then I am ready Harold.

And without any more words we both sat down to a large breakfast, and I had to admit that I had enjoyed the night. The boat was ready for us, and we boarded for Flanders when the sun was already high in the sky.

HAROLD GODWINSON - THE LAST SAXON

FLANDERS

Brugensis came into view long before we were able to draw alongside its busy wharves. The last part of the journey was through a man-made waterway, cut, I was told, in the days of the Romans, to bring the sea to the city. It was slow progress, the sails furled, the oarsmen rowing. The cut was clogged in places by mudbanks that blocked our way, and we were given access by boats which dug a swathe through it. All along its length, there were wharves where small boats pulled alongside buying and selling their goods to local villagers. I understood little of what they said, only catching the odd word which I had picked up from the traders who came to our coastal ports. I had heard much about the place; ships from England as well as the Viking lands were constant visitors. I knew it was highly prized by the Norsemen as well as by England. Not only did it provide a rich source of trade, but offered shelter from the frequent storms that blew along the channel. Flanders was also home to my brother Sweyn

This was my first visit and I hoped to spend some days at the port before setting off to meet with Count Baldwin in Gaunt. I knew that my first meeting with him and with his half-sister Judith, my betrothed, would be awkward, and I wanted to put it off as long as possible. Fortunately, Harold was in no hurry to move on either. There were people he wanted to see; people who could be useful to know; people with secrets to share - for a price. I went with him. He was eager to help me learn the ways of the Flemish traders.

- *Soon, little brother, you will be one of them. And you will need to keep your ears and eyes open. Many of the merchants you see are spies.*

- *Spies? Are you sure?*

HAROLD GODWINSON - THE LAST SAXON

They looked like simple traders with their carts laden with sacks of wool and baskets piled high with leather reins and iron horseshoes. Harold stopped one merchant and inspected the goods in one of the baskets. He held a pair of horseshoes in his hand, weighing them and checking their shape.

- They are not as good as the ones you find in our smithies and forges. But the Scots trade for them.

- Why do they not they come south, to us, to buy the better ones then?

- The Scots prefer to risk the sea crossing and come to Flanders. They hate the English, convinced we will cheat them at every opportunity.

- And are they right?

Harold grinned and patted me on the back.

- We hate the Scots every bit as much as they hate us. So, we will always look to take advantage. You see, little brother, what a funny world it is. And you are soon to be part of it.

I was fed up with the epithet. I have passed my eighteenth year now and should no longer be thought of as Harold's "little brother". I was Tostig Godwinson, soon to be Earl in England and married to a Flemish Count's daughter. I was to become a man of substance.

- I hope you will not continue to call me "little brother" once we arrive at court.

- You will always be "little brother" to me, little brother. But you're right. I shall have to get used to calling you Earl Tostig.

I hoped he would remember. I looked down at the boats and recalled our journey across from England. The sailors had said I was a good omen, and my marriage would be blessed, because the sun shone and there was scarcely more wind than we needed to bring us across the water. I loved being on the deck of a ship. Somehow it felt ingrained into me. I was a sailor, descended from the Vikings and a lover of the sea. And I loved this place. Flanders was a sea-faring country, living and dying by the trade that came up its waters. And I would become part of it by marriage to Judith. I took the picture from my pocket. It was small; a miniature portrait of a strikingly beautiful girl. She was fifteen, now, and would soon be ready for marriage. And who better could she marry than Earl Tostig Godwinson. I had been promised titles stripped from Sweyn, so she would become an English Countess, and Earl Tostig would have friends in high places and foreign lands.

- *Come, little... Tostig. We shall find a place to sleep here tonight, and in the morning, we shall have horses ready for our journey to Gaunt. Judith awaits. And we shall see what mischief our brother has caused here.*

- *Your brother Sweyn has left for Denmark. He stayed here at the court for just a few months, though I offered him a home here. It seems he is a restless spirit.*

It was the countess who spoke, Eleanor of Normandy. I was disappointed. I had hoped to meet up with Sweyn again. But it seems he had got himself into a fight with a Flanders merchant - over the man's wife, we were told. And he had gone, with her, on board a Danish trader, and sailed along the coast.

- *Your brother left under a black cloud, Earl Harold.*
- *Black clouds follow him everywhere he goes.*

- Then I must be sure to avoid him if he returns. There is enough rain here in Flanders without creating even more. This particular black cloud was a woman, the wife of one of our richest merchants. It seems she was flattered to be courted by an English earl.

- He has no titles, and she will find she has no future with my brother.

- In that case I am sorry for both of them, and for her children.

Our night at the port had not been spent without company. Harold invited two Brugensian women to our rooms. I was less clumsy this time, and the woman was more responsive. Standing here in the presence of the countess and her daughter, I felt uncomfortable. Could they tell what I had done? Was it expected anyway? In so many ways I was still the little brother, and I needed to grow up fast. When the Countess spoke, I sensed her eyes boring into my soul, finding all my secrets.

- And now that you see her in the flesh, does Judith please you, Tostig Godwinson?

- She is even more beautiful than the artist has painted her.

It was the reply that we had rehearsed, Harold and I, and it brought a smile to Eleanor's face, and a flush of blood into the cheeks of her daughter. Even had she been ugly as sin, I would have said the same, but Judith was a pretty young woman. Her body was well-formed; her eyes blue; and her hair raven black.

- She carries my Norman blood and colour. And she has a Norman heart too. You will marry a brave, fearless woman, just as her mother is.

I listened to the mother, but I kept my eyes on her daughter, and I saw the cheeks blush again. She would make a fine wife when the time came. Contracts were drawn up, agreements were signed. We would be wed when Judith was eighteen. By then I will be twenty-two and there will be titles and lands.

When we returned to the port, Harold left me free to wander. He was, he said, hunting for information. There were ships from Denmark, carrying men who would have news of Sweyn, as well as news of rebellions and threats to the peace of England.

- *Once you are married, Tostig, you will be our eyes and ears.*
- *Once I am married, Harold, I shall return to England and take up my place in society, part of the nobility.*
- *We shall see, Tostig. Whatever suits England best. You will serve the King in any way he sees fit. And if that is to live here in Flanders then so be it.*

And then he was gone. There was no point arguing with Harold. He would never listen to any opinion but his own. Now Sweyn, if he was here, would be different. *Go your own way,* he had always said. *Take the path that best suits you.* I missed Sweyn. But I had met Hakon, his son. Born from a union with the stolen wife, he had been left behind on the flight to Denmark. A baby boy, innocent of his father's crimes. And now, no better than a homeless orphan. I planned to take Hakon back with us.

I wandered along the port, and then followed a man with a handcart which he was clearly taking to the marketplace. It was a fine wide square, with large wooden tables set out, adorned with flags and signs, each depicting a different type of trader. The man I followed was clearly a wool merchant and he unloaded woollen pelts onto a stall. Even before he had finished unloading his cart he was surrounded by traders. Some were dressed in Viking furs, some in English woollen breeches and tunics, made ornate with shiny metal pins. It was a noisy scene. This was the heart of the city. I was fascinated by the smells coming from one of the stalls in the centre of the market. A small, yellow-skinned man stood shouting at passers-by in a strange language. I stood close by and watched as men and women bought oils and ointments and potions, and rich dark spices, yellows, reds and browns which gave off delicious smells. I recognised the peppers that hung from strings attached to the stall. I remembered their sharp hot taste when mother had put them into our stews. Brugensis was a fascinating place. A meeting place for all of the traders and a melting pot for all the stratagems and plots to overthrow kings and countries. It was dark before Harold returned. I had gone to my room at the tavern - alone this time. To have taken a woman tonight would have seemed like a betrayal of Judith, though I doubted I would sleep alone every night until she came to England. But tonight, my head was full of sights and sounds, of senses and tastes, and I was glad to be in Flanders.

- *He must not be allowed to return.*
Harold was adamant and King Edward was in full agreement. Sweyn had arrived home ahead of us. He had met with our father and together they had gone to the king to plead his cause. But the king saw treachery everywhere. This was hardly surprising, given the dangerous road he had had to travel to sit on the throne. There really

were enemies everywhere, but our father worked hard to show the loyalty of the Godwins. And Sweyn, he assured the king, was no threat.

- *I served loyally under Cnut, and I shall always support his heirs and kin. As the mighty Cnut's stepson, you will always have my fealty.*

The king was not convinced.

- *You are your son's father. I can count upon your support so long as it suits the Godwin clan. Your allegiance is not in doubt. Your allegiance can be bought and sold like any commodity in a Flanders market. It is your heart and your soul I question, Godwin.*

- *I have always looked for a Saxon King to rule over Saxon England. And you, Edward, are in a direct line from the greatest of them all, King Alfred himself. King Alfred's seed will always find, in me and my sons, loyalty and support that befits such a noble line.*

The king smiled, but he would have his way.

- *Your nephew Beorn had spoken for him, and now you come to plead his case. But your son Sweyn has no loyal bones in his body. He betrayed me and I banished him to Flanders. He betrayed Count Baldwin and moved on to Denmark. There he betrayed Estridsen and now he seeks to return home...*

- *There were misunderstandings, your Majesty, unspecified. No charges were brought against him.*

- *A woman again, I have no doubt.*

- *The boy is a fool, but not a treacherous one.*

-*Tell that to Beorn. His own cousin; a man who supported his cause, and a man who was murdered by him. Despite your wife's strongest denial, still he claims to be the son of Cnut. He challenges my right, Godwin. He challenges me.*

- *The boy has too much ambition.*

HAROLD GODWINSON - THE LAST SAXON

- Sweyn is not a boy. He is a man who must be responsible for the bad decisions he continues to make. He is a niðing, a nothing, a man of no honour. This ambition you speak of will drive him to plot my death. I know he is your son, and I value your loyalty, Godwin, but he must leave England. He has sinned not just against man, but against God. He must leave these shores, give up this nonsense of his parentage, and do proper penance before I can consider his return. And as for you, Godwin, it is not for nothing you are known as the Kingmaker. Cnut was grateful to have you at his side, but do not think I will be as generous as he was to your kin. If you cross me, if you betray England... Do not think that your daughter's marriage has bought you privileges that blind me to your true thoughts. I respect you as my wife's father, but you must continue to earn my respect as my loyal earl.

Throughout the journey home, our father's shoulders drooped, and his head was bowed. But Harold seemed to grow a little straighter. He resented father's blind support of the eldest son. Later, back in Senlac, as we ate around the oak table Harold spoke with our father. I listened in dismay. Would I never see Sweyn again?

- He must not be allowed to return. We must be careful, father. If we bind ourselves too closely to my errant brother, it will go badly for us.

- He is not a bad son...

- No, he is a foolish one. And his foolishness leaves us all exposed. The king fears his treachery and we shall be held accountable for it. I feel the thread that keeps us safe growing thinner. He will make it snap altogether and we shall be cast adrift. Then you shall have wasted all those years, clawing back what our grandfather lost. We are earls, respected and feared. We must hold on tight to our power.

HAROLD GODWINSON - THE LAST SAXON

Mother spoke up for Sweyn and cried when Harold spoke. But she knew it was in vain. Godwin was a good man. Despite all the rumours of her oldest boy's parentage, her husband still fought for him. But the fight was over. Sweyn would leave in the morning. The king had commanded it, and Harold had got his way. Mother dried her tears and spoke quietly.

- *The king has given him a chance to show his true heart. He has told him to do penance. He must make a pilgrimage. Or else he shall be banished again to Flanders never to return. And what of Hakon? What will happen to his son?*
- *The bastard boy will return to Flanders. He will be safe there. Judith has vowed to protect him. He will not inherit our name, but he will not be damned by his father's deeds.*

At least in Flanders I shall have a chance to meet the boy again. And perhaps his father too. As Earl Tostig, with a Flemish wife, Flanders would be safer than England.

Edith The Fair

HAROLD GODWINSON - THE LAST SAXON

HANDFASTED

Edith the Fair. That's how I'm known, though, in truth, I have never discovered if the epithet relates to my overall beauty, which I hope to be the case, or the colour of my hair, which on some days, those I call the rebellious days, resembles dry straw. But for whatever reason they use it, I am known as Edith the Fair. I never thought to ask, in case I received the wrong answer! I would rather be known as The Gentle Swan, which has been loosely translated from my family name: Swanneschals. But I shall settle for Edith the Fair. Of course, what I should really be called is Lady Godwinson, but there are many in England who will not recognise the 'handfasting' ritual as a true marriage. Harold, to be fair to him, treats me as his true wife, and expects others to do so. But there are concerns about our children's future place in the world, and then there is the edict from Rome.

Harold and I were brought together in the first year of King Edward's reign. I was an ideal match for him, and he was a strong, tall man with whom I would, I felt sure, fall in love. The lands around Walsingham, where I had lived for all of my twenty-one years, were presented as a dowry and I suspect that Harold saw that, as much as me, as a prize worth having. And the marriage was arranged. I had met and got to know Harold Godwinson some years ago, when I was just a child of seven and he seemed already grown up, though only three years my senior. Even then he was taller than the other boys his age, and, like most of the girls from the area to me Harold was a god. Tall, fair, strong. Earl Godwin and my father talked together at that first encounter, long into the night, and it was agreed that he and I would be a perfect match. Mother had told me, and I wore a smirk on my face for weeks, long after the Godwins had returned home. In truth, I had wondered whether it was Sweyn that I would be coupled with. Sweyn was a little older, but there was something in his countenance that made me glad it was not him. So, Harold and I were betrothed.

He and I would meet, with mother as a chaperone, every six months or so. I always felt as though the Godwins were coming to check up on their goods, but Harold and I spent time together and I always found him to be kindly, considerate and growing more handsome. We walked and talked together, striding across the flat fens and Harold seemed to enjoy those days of our childhood. Much of my time in those early days was spent in the holy house at Walsingham, where an old monk was assigned to teach me to read and write. I learned to create the illustrated pages to accompany the stories that were so familiar to me. My tuition was paid for by Earl Godwin, though my father was well able to afford it. It was Godwin's way of showing his commitment to me, and he expected my studies to bear fruit.

- Edith must be able to help my son with his work. She must learn to read and write, as befits the wife of an earl, and a member of the Godwinson household.

The years passed by in this way. I learned much more than my Christian studies. Harold's father had not always been so well-placed. Before King Cnut, Godwin was banished, through the treachery of his father. Harold had told me the story and the lesson he had learned.

- We must do all we can to stay in the king's good graces. I will never want this family to face such banishment again. We are to be known always as the king's trusted servants, and in that way retain our own *position as the most important family in the land - second only to the king.*

- And I am to be part of that family?

- We will be wed, Edith. Then you will bask in the glory of the Godwinson name.

Harold's father, Godwin, was by now well into his middle age. Harold carried out many of the duties as Earl, and the marriage was planned to be held at Senlac, on my eighteenth birthday, from which date my dowry could be offered, but the Godwinsons were in chaos. There had been rumours, spread willingly by Harold's elder brother himself, that Sweyn was son of King Cnut, born from their mother's dalliance with the king. It was denied - in a court in London, father said - and the story was suppressed, but there were some who still believed it. Harold and Godwin felt the marriage should be put off until all such talk was forgotten. Then it was announced that Edith, Harold's sister, would be married to King Edward himself. Suddenly plans were laid for our own marriage.

- As my wife you will attend the wedding as sister-in-law of the queen. You will have a place at her side at court. The Godwinsons will have even greater influence.

It wasn't the most romantic proposal, but I believed we were ready for marriage. I had already waited three years and so plans were laid. It would be a handfasting; a wedding without a celebrant. It was common enough, especially when couples had to marry in a hurry; usually there was a baby on the way. Not in our case. For us the hurry was the King's wedding. We would have the ceremony and later, probably at the Cathedral in Winchester, we would have the Christian wedding I was promised.

HAROLD GODWINSON - THE LAST SAXON

Handfasting was familiar enough to me. I had attended, as guest of honour, a number of such marriages in the towns and villages. And my handfasting was a lavish affair, despite the lack of a Christian celebrant. My mother herself had been handfasted to my father, and they had seen no need to formalise the arrangement.

- It is part of our tradition - to be married in the Danish way. We are all Saxons now, but our history is from the colder northern lands. Handfasting was the way of our mothers and fathers, and of their mothers and fathers. You are part of a long tradition.

And so, it was settled. The journey to Senlac, undertaken in Spring, should not be one of hardship especially for a bride waiting to meet her groom. But, for me, it was a journey of some trepidation. I had not fully considered how life as a married woman would be. The physical side of the marriage was an unknown world, and listening to my mother on the cart that took us ever closer to my husband-to-be, I began to feel what all betrothed women must feel. Would I know what to do? Would I please my husband? Would it hurt? It was this last question that worried me most, if I am to be honest. Listening to my mother describing such intimacy, and hearing her description of the act itself… But I was comforted by the fact that I was not the first woman to be in such a place. Down all the way from Eve, our first mother, women must have trembled and feared that first night.

- And what of Harold, mother? Will he feel the same?

- Harold will have experience. All men come to marriage with experience and expect their women to be pure. Such is the way of things.

- And from where, from whom, will this experience have come?

- There are women who give themselves to men - usually for money - and no doubt Harold will have slept with one or more.

HAROLD GODWINSON - THE LAST SAXON

- Really?

- He will be the experienced partner. He will help you through that first time that women fear so much.

I acted coy, but I knew of such women and of such practices. I was not as innocent as my mother would believe.   I tried not to think about Harold being so intimate with another woman. I drew a little comfort from the way my mother described it - as a sort of transaction.   This was not love.   There was no need for jealousy. Rather, I should be grateful that, as a consequence of such coupling, Harold would be better prepared for me.

We held hands, Harold and I. Our two mothers, Harold's and mine, standing facing us, held the braided gold and silver cord above our hands; slowly they lowered it so that I could feel the tassels tickling my wrist. Harold spoke his oath slowly and deliberately, without a single quiver in his voice. I could feel my mouth frame the words he spoke, as we had rehearsed them often enough. Then it was my turn to speak the familiar words.

- In the joining of our hands, held fast by the knot that binds them, so are our lives bound together. This cord binds us to our vow.

My mother then lifted our hands and showed them to the guests who stood behind us:

- By this cord you are bound to your vows taken here today. May the knot remain tied so long as your love shall last. May this cord draw your hands together in love, never to be used in anger.

HAROLD GODWINSON - THE LAST SAXON

Gently, the two mothers laid the cord across our joined hands and then tied a simple knot beneath. Cheers and whoops filled the room. The two mothers stood apart and opened a 'doorway' through which we could pass, and as we walked, leaves of myrtle and lavender were sprinkled over us. We were handfasted. Harold and I were man and wife. I had always assumed that later, perhaps after the royal wedding, we would have the marriage formalised, Christianised, though it wasn't the case.

The feasting that followed went long into the night. I longed for it to go on forever, enjoying being the centre of attention while also putting off the moment I had feared. Then the lighted rushes in the corners of the room were doused, the air turned smoky, and darkness returned to the hall. It was time. There was no putting it off. Harold and I were escorted to our bedroom, led by Sweyn carrying a flame to light the way. And there we were left, with plenty of laughter and back-slapping. I stood in the room, looking at the bed. There was a linen sheet, covered with furs.

- *There will be little need for the furs, Edith. I shall keep you warm. Our bodies pressed together will give us all the heat we need.*

I giggled. He started to undress, and I tugged at the lace of my bodice, watching him. His body was naked now, standing in front of me, holding out his hands to me, while I fumbled with laces, my hands clumsy. His body was as beautiful as I had imagined it would be. His hands came to mine, and held mine steady, and together we worked until I too stood naked. Then he lifted me up, and with a single swing of his arms laid me on my back on the bed. My eyes were closed, and I was afraid.

There had been no need for fear. My husband was as gentle as he was beautiful. He had whispered to me as we lay together, and his voice was comforting and before I knew it, our bodies had joined together. What pain I'd felt was momentary. In the morning Harold and I went together to break our fast, and his hand held mine nestled in his, so that all could see we belonged together. I was married. I was a woman now, and soon I would be a member of the royal household in attendance at the King's wedding in London. His sister, my namesake, born in the same year as I, would be Queen of England.

Godwin's mother, it seems, had been the driving force behind our ceremony, and my parents had been happy to oblige the Earl's wife. Gytha Thorkelsdottir was Danish, both by birth and inclination. Her father and brothers still held lands and titles there.

- *All our weddings were like this, done 'the Danish way'. It was in the days before we were all so very Christian! Handfasting is a tradition and you and my son have carried on that tradition. It is part of the old ways.*

But we were in England now, and when I felt the first kicks of the baby inside me, I wondered if it would matter that there had been no Christian celebrant to bless our union. Harold did his best to reassure me:

- *If it was good enough for Harefoot to inherit the throne then surely handfasted parentage can be no disadvantage.*

But times were changing, and this new king had different ideas. So, I shall probably always be known as Edith the Fair, and not by my husband's title.

HAROLD GODWINSON - THE LAST SAXON

SPY

Edward had been on the throne three years when he married my sister-in-law. Not for them a simple handfasting ceremony. It was a grand affair, held on the very spot where Edward had earlier been crowned, in the great cathedral of St Paul, standing in the centre of the city of London. And - as my father told me - she would be crowned Queen of England, which was rare indeed. The king's line was Saxon; he was a descendant of Ethelred, and his speech in the Abbey made it clear he would honour that lineage and restore the royal house to bear the Wessex name. Harold and I were to become members of the royal household, not just by marriage of Edith to the king, but because Earls of Wessex now had powerful protection and honours. I was a Wessex bride, a woman of honour.

Harold was eager for me to remain at the queen's side. From her I could access the king's mind.

- You mean act as a spy?

- I mean that it is wise to be prepared.

- A spy in the court?

- We have to maintain our position close to the king. There are many among us who seek to replace us, usurp our position. We want to be certain that what the king hears are our words, and that what he knows we know.

So, there it was. I was to be a spy. I did broach the issue of our wedding, but Harold was often away, and my words missed their mark. But I was Harold Godwinson's wife and spying was a small price to pay. After all, I reasoned, my own security and that of my family, depends entirely now on my husband's position.

HAROLD GODWINSON - THE LAST SAXON

When I felt the first kicks of the baby it was difficult to suppress a smile. Not only would I have the pleasure of my own child, but surely Harold would realise that the best way to secure the rights for his son was through a Christian marriage. But Harold, on one of those brief visits home, refused to speak of it. He was happy that he would have an heir - and was certain that this young child would inherit his land and titles.

- *The king will not deny us. Our son… for I know in my bones it is a boy, will become a Wessex Earl, like his father and grandfather before him, linked by blood and title to the kings of England.*

And that was it. No further discussion.

Harold had been called back to London. There was talk everywhere of rebellion, and King Edward meant to suppress it, and to reinforce his borders. The king had called a summit.

- *Magnus - in Norway - means to win back England. He means to spread the Viking lands and resume control over England. I have worked hard to re-establish my father's line. England will not become Viking again, subject to Danelaw and punitive taxation. And you, my earls will not want them robbing you of your lands and titles.*

The rumours then were true. England was under threat of invasion. It was Harold who spoke first at the meeting, standing alongside Godwin, his father. The other earls looked to him, with his special kinship to the throne, to speak on their behalf. Godwin himself, not the strong vigorous man he had been, looked to his son, now his heir, to speak for them all.

HAROLD GODWINSON - THE LAST SAXON

- *Let them come, Edward. Our forces are ready to repel them. Magnus can barely hold on to his own lands. This invasion is beyond him.*

- *He has made a pact with others who see England as a prize. Not least Harald Sigurdsson, Norway's king. They hate each other but they would gladly join together to seize these lands as part of any future peace deal between them. We must keep the Viking kings away. Let them know we are not to be taken lightly. Let them realise it is safer for them to fight each other than to fight the Saxon army we shall raise.*

- *And what do you want from us?*

- *Your loyalty first, Godwinson.*

- *That you have, King Edward. No family could be more loyal. It was through my father that you became king, and through his son you shall remain so.*

- *You, Harold Godwinson, I grant the title Earl of East Anglia. You are already established in the region in your wife's name and titles, so you will want to defend it well.*

- *And in doing so I shall defend the country from Eastern invaders.*

So, there it was. Harold was to become the most powerful of all the earls. When Godwin died, he would inherit Wessex and then the Godwinsons would have sway over all the land from the western peninsular to the Wash. Second only to the king, indeed. And I, Edith, would be part of this life. And our children would carry the line far into the future. Surely now he would consent to formalising our union. For a moment I even pictured myself as Queen of England. Could Harold raise himself so high?

There were rumours of another sort too. Especially in our own household. Queen Edith was a regular visitor to Senlac. A year after her marriage we were all surprised to see that, unlike her sister-in-law, she was not carrying an heir.

- *It is different for a queen, Edith,* she told me. *The king is busy ensuring the safety of his kingdom. And I am left too often alone.*

- *As am I, sister. Your brother is too frequently in London or about your husband's business, but he still has found time…*

Queen Edith looked at my belly, and I could sense the longing in her. She took my hand and led me away from the others and in the chamber that was still kept for her return visits, we sat together. When she spoke, she held my hands in hers.

- *I envy you, Edith. I wish that I too was carrying a child. I am ready in my heart but unfortunately the King has forsworn our marriage bed. He has taken a vow of celibacy. There can be no child.*

Later, in our own bedroom, when I told Harold what she had said, he laughed - a loud and raucous sound that would have echoed even into his sister's bedroom.

- *The king says that. I fancy he has a desire to be a saintly man, like his uncle. But he lacks the courage for martyrdom. Instead, he takes holy vows; he claims celibacy, but I have stories I could tell. My sister will lose nothing from this. Her power remains intact; our power remains intact. Other spies tell me he has chosen this path to avoid further links with us. Despite all we have done to put him on his throne, still he does not trust us. No, I think the king has motives that go beyond his own sainthood.*

- *But our sister will have no child. And Edward shall have no true heir. Will that not lead to chaos and fighting, and a greater chance that the Danes and Norwegians will come here?*

HAROLD GODWINSON - THE LAST SAXON

- My dearest Edith. The wind blows in our favour. I am the queen's protector. Sweyn cannot be trusted with such a role. And if I am the queen's protector then perhaps...

Harold put his hands on my lips. I was to say nothing more.

- Leave the Viking raiders to us. We shall match them. We shall never give England back to the Vikings. England will remain a Saxon country. For eternity. You have done well, Edith. This is the best news. And while I know you feel, as a woman with a tender heart must feel, some sympathy for our sister, this news is good news for our family.

When baby Godwin was born, in the fourth year of King Edward's reign, Senlac became a welcome haven from the palace. I put aside gathering and sharing information about the king and concentrated on our baby boy. Named for his grandfather, the old man doted on him. My father-in-law was happy to lay down affairs of state, though he still commanded much respect and honour from the king. Instead, he spent time, along with my mother-in-law bouncing baby Godwin on his knee. It was only later that I realised it was all about "affairs of state". This boy would inherit not just titles but the role of kingmaker, unless of course... Harold made it clear that there was still a job to be done.

- Sweyn has been sent to Wales to crush the rebellion there. The king knows he needs the sons of Godwin to keep him safe. We have been called to Westminster to meet with The Witan. The king must relinquish some of his power, give it to the earls who better represent

the people. And we are to be installed as principal advisers; not members of the Witan itself but involved in the parliament.

- And am I recalled too? I wanted more time with baby Godwin. He was too young to be separated from his mother.

- Where else should you be but by your husband's side? My mother has arranged for a wet-nurse for the boy. The king likes you; he is charmed by your piety and seduced by your father's wealth. He has especially asked for you to join me.

Was Edith the Fair so important to her king and her country? Or was this more plotting by my husband? Either way, the decision was made. I had no say in it.

- It has never been more important than now to have you close to Queen Edith. She trusts you.

And there lay the problem. The queen did trust me, and every day I betrayed her.

- Our brother, Sweyn, has once again set himself against the king.

- What has he done this time? I knew enough about Harold's eldest brother to know that he too frequently risked all that his father had attained, and now risked Harold's hard-earned position at court. Harold could scarcely conceal the rage he felt.

- He has stolen away with the Abbess of Leominster, thinking in that way to adopt the lands and titles she holds. The king is furious. He sees it as another plot of the Wessex Earls to steal power from him. He has been banished. I need to know if more is planned against us as punishment for my brother's folly? We must be prepared.

And so, once again, I found myself at Queen Edith's side, eyes and ears open. And my baby boy was in Senlac being nursed by a stranger.

HAROLD GODWINSON - THE LAST SAXON

Edmund was born a year later. I was back in Senlac for his birth, and my mother was with me. Harold had gone to Flanders to find news of his brother and he had taken Tostig with him. Tostig was to be betrothed to Judith, the Count's half-sister and Harold acted on his father's behalf to ensure the match was appropriate - that is, the union would bring political and financial benefits to us. When Harold and Tostig arrived, Sweyn had already moved on. It seemed he had betrayed the Count's trust and he had fled again, this time to Denmark. The story had it that he had got into a fight with a trader, and then fled with the man's wife. But the fact that it was to Denmark he had gone, would raise the king's suspicions, bringing back all the old stories of his birth. It was too much. Sweyn was a fool, but a dangerous one.

Young Edmund was so different from his brother. Godwin bore all the traits of his father's family: the russet hair, curly and coarse; the bold chin, and pale face. His little brother was fair, like me, with straight hair that was always unruly. The face was rounder, and he always had rosy cheeks. The boys were very different, but they were both such good boys. They allowed themselves to be petted and cuddled, and while Godwin's face seemed stern and serious, Edmund was a happy laughing baby. The boys were my life.

Though I saw little of Harold in those days, and we spent so much time apart, my third boy arrived less than a year later. We named him Magnus, more for my mother's line than his father's. The family was made even larger by the addition of Hakon, Sweyn's boy, left behind in Antwerp, when his father fled. Hakon was the same age as Godwin. It was Tostig who had brought him back to Senlac.

But my days at court soon resumed. Queen Edith looked at our growing family with more than a little envy. The king and queen had separate bedrooms and she had little concourse with him. Not only was she denied children, but she was also denied the warmth of a husband's body next to hers. Of course, he was almost twenty years older than her, but the king was still a vigorous and attractive man, and she genuinely loved him. I felt for her, but remembered Harold's words. So long as they remained childless, our children would sit closer to the throne. I couldn't imagine what circumstances would bring us to such a place, but I understood how important it was that we should not be usurped of our power. Queen Edith and I spent much of our time walking together, hands held, like young maids gossiping about life at court.

- *Our brother, Sweyn, continues to make life difficult for all of us. When his boy was brought back to England, I asked the king if he could come to the palace. If I couldn't have children of my own, then perhaps I could be a mother to my nephew. But the king would not hear of it. He still thinks that Sweyn is after his crown. He thinks he means to chop off his head, just as our father chopped off the head of the king's own brother, Alfred.*
- *We are all the king's loyal servants, your majesty.*
- *I know my brothers, Edith. Better than you. I grew up with their scheming. They are my father's sons and will never rest until...* The queen stopped short of accusing her father and brothers of treason. So, I finished for her.
- *Until the king is safe from all his enemies. They will do nothing to harm him. We are all the king's family now.*
- *You must know, sister-in-law, that the king has a long memory. He remembers the wrongs that were done to him and his family - by our father. Now, he will never let down his guard.*

This was nothing new. Harold knew this already. But perhaps there was something I, even though a mere woman, could do to ease the tensions between us.

- So. what would it take, your majesty? To convince the king that we are loyal and want no more than to serve him well?

- Sweyn must be kept away. It is Sweyn that the king fears most. This story of his birth rankles with him.

- Harold will not let him return.   Sweyn is not a threat to your husband, Edith.

The queen smiled. She knew Harold and his machinations.

- My brother will have some benefit from Sweyn's absence, I think. The lands that Sweyn holds will pass to him, no doubt.

There was nothing to be gained from protesting. The queen was right. She knew Harold well enough. Plans had already been made to take all his lands and titles to himself. Sweyn's loss was to be Harold's gain. The queen had new information.

- Sweyn is on his way here, to see the king at the court. He has offered to change his ways. He will lay down his sword and swear his fealty oath again. My father will support him.

This was news to me. Godwin himself would plead for his eldest son! Harold must be told.

HAROLD GODWINSON - THE LAST SAXON

EXILE

When mud gets thrown about, inevitably some of it sticks. And there was plenty of mud. Sweyn had attracted much of it and Godwin's name was no longer as trusted as it was. And when the father is besmirched, you can be sure the sons (and daughters-in-law) will smell it on themselves too. Harold told me, and often repeated it, that, to survive in this king's favour, we had to be sure that our enemies were bought off or disappeared. I never sought clarification. Perhaps I should have asked him exactly what he meant, but I am not naive. There are many ways to disappear; being out of the king's sight made you invisible. It didn't take a scholar to realise that making someone disappear was easy when you have power and wealth. But we were not alone in seeing this as a solution; Harold was right about that. There were many in England at that time who fought to get closer to the king. Harold's suspicions were aroused when the king, suddenly, out of the blue, sent for him. Edward, in his new righteous colours, took sides with the Holy Roman Emperor when Count Baldwin of Flanders, an erstwhile ally, took up arms against him. The war had been raging for four years now, and regular reports showed that Flanders despite having some early success against Henry's armies had lost control of Valenciennes. Harold would have preferred, I think, to take up arms in support of Flanders, but King Edward was of a different mind. Harold set sail to join with the armies of the emperor.

- *Get close to the king and queen while I am away, Edith. Make sure we know what is in the king's mind. No thought should be spoken that I do not know.*

HAROLD GODWINSON - THE LAST SAXON

The role of spy never sat easily with me. I liked my sister-in-law, the queen, and I felt I was betraying her. But I knew my duty. My husband and our children came first, and I would stay close and listen.

- *Surely, our sister will not let anything come between us, her family and him?*
- *Edith is the queen. She will do as she is commanded. No. It is you, Edith, I trust. Stay close.*
- *And what of your brother? What is to be done about Sweyn?*
- *My father is adamant. He will take his case to the court. But I will never return his titles or land. Sweyn may find a home here, but he will never regain his place.*

There was no more to be said. Once Harold dismissed a topic, it was done. He spent the last few days with us at Senlac. The boys were growing boisterous now, and Harold encouraged their play. But when he left, he did so with clear instructions.

- *These boys of ours must not spend all their time at play, Edith. They will need to have the skills of statesmen as well as soldiers. Find them tutors, and make sure they study hard. I shall see how much they have benefited when I return.* And then he was gone. There were monks a-plenty who would have gladly taken on the prestigious role of tutor to the house of Godwin, but it was to my own tutors I returned. I trusted them, and they were loyal to me. The boys were in good hands.

Sweyn returned three days after Harold had sailed. I suspected that his timing was deliberate. Though he was older and more gnarled, Sweyn was no match for his determined younger brother.- *You missed your brother, Sweyn. Harold has gone to join the emperor's war.*

HAROLD GODWINSON - THE LAST SAXON

- At the King's behest I have no doubt.- He is a loyal servant, Sweyn. The House of Godwin has always been loyal to their kings.

- My father was called 'the kingmaker'. I have no doubt that Harold has similar ambitions. Or even higher office perhaps?

Godwin and Gytha, my mother-in-law, had ridden south to meet with Sweyn, and parents and son spent time locked away together. But secrets are difficult to keep here at Senlac; and especially so when I have become such an accomplished spy. Godwin, Gytha and Sweyn were to seek an audience with the king, and work to regain Sweyn's place in the king's court. Titles and lands could come later. The first task would be to have Sweyn back in England. But Gytha was blind to Sweyn's faults. She worshipped her eldest son, despite the charges he had made of her infidelity. She believed that he could change, that he had changed. I suspect that Godwin knew better, but Sweyn was his eldest son, his heir, and he wanted to have him back at Senlac. And Beorn would ride with them - Godwin's nephew, cousin to Harold and his brothers. They would seek a pardon. I left the boys with their grandmother and strict instructions as to their routines, journeying to London to meet with Queen Edith.

- What will the king do, Edith? Will He grant a pardon to Sweyn?

- My eldest brother is a fool. He has ever been a fool. A man whose head is turned by a neat ankle and curly hair. The king doesn't trust him.

- He will refuse our father's request?

- I think he is minded to give Sweyn a final chance. But I cannot predict which way this will fall. A wife learns much of her husband's mind in the bedroom, and we have not shared a bedroom, the king and I, for some years. He has forsworn any consummation of our marriage. I cannot tell you his mind.

- But you think he may grant a pardon? You and Gytha are close, Edith. She adores her eldest son, even after all his errors. For her sake perhaps, you will make the case to the king?
- I have spoken with him. I hope he has listened. I have pleaded for him and for his son, for Hakon. Sweyn must give up, once and for all, this nonsense he talks about his lineage. That is what King Edward will demand.

Whatever Godwin said; however, Edith pleaded; whether promises were extracted from Sweyn, none of this is known. But King Edward welcomed Sweyn back and together we all returned to Senlac to celebrate. I knew that Harold would be unhappy with the outcome. Sweyn was a dangerous brother. It would only be a matter of time before his wayward nature would show itself again. But for now, the family was together - except for Harold himself, who was still fighting the emperor's wars. I wrote him letters, and letters were returned.
Let Sweyn have his head. He will not be able to resist his true nature. We shall see. He shall not be in England for long.
For Hakon's sake I was happy. The boy was growing up, and it was good for him to have contact with his father. Beorn, for his part, though he interceded on Sweyn's behalf, was as set as Harold. He would give up none of the land and titles that had come to him from Sweyn's exile. Sweyn thanked them all, over and over again, but his heart was not in it. He came to me one night, thinking to profit from Harold's absence. I had just retired to my bedroom and was unpinning my hair.

- If I were my brother, I should never have left you here on your own.
Undefended.

He moved closer and I could smell the ale on his breath.

- I feel well-enough protected, Sweyn.

- Edith the Fair! How justified is that name!

I cringed at his flattery. I could see where this was leading.

- I carry a knife with me, Sweyn. For any eventualities…

and I drew the knife from the special sheath I had had sewn into the
sleeve.

- …so, you see, I am well-protected.

He smiled, a leer really, and backed off a little.

- You are a true Godwin, I see. My brother has set you against me.

- Your actions, and your nature have set me against you, Sweyn.
Nothing else.

- You will not speak for me to Harold? You will not ask him to return
my lands and titles?

- Those lands and titles will pass to my sons, Sweyn. I shall make no
such request. And I shall say nothing of your visit here tonight. That
may spare your life.

- And what of my son? What of Hakon? What will become of him?

- You care little for the boy, Sweyn. Here he is loved, and he will
benefit from our protection, despite what his father does to dishonour
his - and our - name.

The smile was gone. In its place was anger.

- I shall have them back. All my titles. All my land. I shall take them
by force.

- Harold would not let you. He is not afraid of his elder brother. And
he has the king's love.

HAROLD GODWINSON - THE LAST SAXON

- Huh! The king has no love for the Godwins. He will turn on us soon enough. Harold and Beorn have opposed me at every turn. They have benefited from my banishment and now they refuse to give up what is mine, what will be my son's.

- Harold and Beorn know you too well, Sweyn. They have no fear of you. Harold says of you: 'Give him just enough rope and with it he will make his own noose'.

Sweyn turned on his heel and slammed the door behind him. I stood in the silence that followed. I was shaking, and I hoped he had not seen it. I replaced the dagger into its sheath. I had never drawn it before, never felt the need, but now I was grateful to Harold for making me cautious.

News of Beorn's murder reached us just three days later. I immediately sent the news to Harold.

It seems that your cousin was persuaded to meet with Sweyn at Bosham. There were men there, your brother's men, who captured him and set him aboard a ship to Dartmouth, chained and bound. There Sweyn did his best to persuade him to return the lands - I leave, dear husband, to your imagination the nature of this persuasion. Beorn's body was returned to Senlac. He has been buried with all honour. And Sweyn has sailed away from Dartmouth. Is there no end to your brother's treachery? Beorn spoke for him to the king! And this is how he is repaid.

Harold returned to Senlac later that month. It was autumn, and the war between the Count and Henry was not going well. The heavy rains brought a truce of sorts, but nothing had been decided. The two armies were exhausted and there was a lull. Harold, at first, seemed happy to be home, but his content was short-lived. My husband was a soldier, who was never happier than when engaged in war.

The news of Archbishop Eadsige's death hit us hard. Eadsige had been a loyal friend of Godwin and Godwin's own land holdings grew under his time in high office.   Godwin, and later his sons, had always seen him as an ally, and while they were not great churchmen themselves, they believed in the appointment of a Saxon prelate to be Archbishop of Canterbury. With him there, the whole country, all its leaders, clerical and lay, were Saxon, by birth or inclination. I had spent much time with the old man, enjoying his wisdom and company. When he fell ill, I went to be with him at Canterbury. His death led to bad times for us. The king, doubtless persuaded by his mother, appointed Robert of Jumieges, a Norman prior from Rouen. Harold spoke for all of us.

- *This is Emma. I see her hand in this. She means to have England overrun with Normans. First the archbishop, then a king. The bastard Duke William has his eyes on England, and she would give it to him. With no Saxon heir we are all to become Normans.*

His words reached King Edward. It seems we were not the only ones with spies. Godwin was summoned - alone - into the king's presence.

- *We have removed your pet Archbishop from office, Godwin. In his place we have a man who has no love for your family. You have grown fat under Eadsige. My new Archbishop has told me of your disdain for him and for my mother. You should expect leaner times. It was Robert who led me down the paths of righteousness when we were exiled in Normandy. That exile was all your doing. Now I aim to repay you.*

Godwin returned to Senlac with the bad news. We were to be exiled. This was the king's revenge. All of us: Godwin, his sons and their families; all to be sent abroad. Except of course, for Queen Edith. She was to be sent to a nunnery. The king, childless, hoped to divorce her, and rid himself of the Godwin connection. The old man seemed broken, but it was Harold who spoke up. His face had that look I knew so well. He was defiant. He was angry. And he would seek revenge. The king would learn what it was to cross Harold Godwinson.

- We have more rights to be here than the king himself. We are Saxon earls, and English blood runs through our veins. The king will learn that we are not some vassals to be discarded at will. We will raise an army. We will die before we are forced off our lands.

Senlac, our home, was abandoned. We were not safe here. An army raised by the Earls of Mercia and Northumbria, whose eyes were set firmly on the lands and titles of Godwin's heirs, would carry out the king's orders, and would harry us from England. We fled to my old home and received support there. There were many men who owed allegiance to the Wessex earls, and whose fortunes would wane if we were exiled. These men were called to support us, and before long there was an army ready to march on London. I took the boys with me, including Hakon, to the church at Walsingham, claiming sanctuary. We were safe there. I was known and loved for my family's sake, and Walsingham became our new home. Godwin led the army, Harold and Tostig on either side. Sweyn did not ride with them. The harshest judgement fell onto him, despite the queen's strongest entreaties, Sweyn would never be allowed to return. He was already on his way back to Flanders. He announced that he would take a pilgrimage to Jerusalem, in repentance for all his sins. We never saw him again. Harold would be his father's heir and I knew this was what he had strived for ever since his birth; ever since fate had had him born one son too late!

HAROLD GODWINSON - THE LAST SAXON

GODWIN

By any measure, my father-in-law, Godwin, Earl of Wessex, was a successful man. He had climbed his way (over God knows how many dead bodies) to the top of the tree. His daughter was the crowned Queen of England, and his second son was almost as powerful as he himself. I can only imagine then what it must be like to fall from such a height. Times were changing at court. The Norman influences from the king's mother were growing stronger and the king's closest advisers spoke in Norman tongue now. The memory of his father's, Wulfnoth's, fall still hung heavy on him. He had worked hard to bring the clan back to favour. And now, it seemed, it had all been for nothing.

The rebellion in Dover had been the flint that had started the fire. King Edward, taking the side of the Count of Boulogne, ordered Godwin to punish the people of Dover, for opposing the French invasion. Godwin considered taking action. He was reluctant but he knew it might be the only way to retain his place in court. Harold refused the order.

- *I shall not punish Saxon men for opposing the Boulogne force. The King must see that this is a Saxon land. He is too easily swayed by his Norman mother.*

Harold could be as flexible in his ways as his father. But he held on tighter to the principle that the King of England must uphold the Saxon ways and must resist other people seeking to claim rights and territory here. He was able to persuade his father – no easy feat. Their refusal led to their fall; it also gave them valuable allies. But they could not stay in England. I was safe enough at Walsingham, but Godwin and Tostig sought refuge in Flanders, and were joined there by Sweyn. Harold went to Dublin. He had allies there, people who would support him, people who would help raise an army. So, while his father sat in exile in Flanders it was Harold who raised the force. Godwin returned with Tostig, to join the rebel army, though Sweyn was now on his way to Jerusalem.

- *We are stronger without him. Sweyn has left a trail of bad blood wherever he has been. Let him make his peace with God, while we seek to regain our place with the king.*

News reached us in Walsingham of the king's surrender. It was never spoken in such terms, of course it wasn't. We were reunited at Senlac and life settled again, but we were uneasy. Edward was a capricious king, bending with the wind, one moment swearing allegiance to his Saxon roots, and then succumbing to his mother's pleas to turn England into a Norman kingdom.

- *We must do what we can to ensure the king resists that woman's influence. But Edward must save face. He cannot be seen to be weak, even in the face of superior forces. He will require some movement on our side. He will need to show us that there is a price to pay. And I am already working on that. We have agreed to the permanence of Sweyn's banishment. With Sweyn safely in Jerusalem…*

- *Will he not return here once he is back from his pilgrimage?*

- *Sweyn will never return, Edith.*

There was a tone in these words that I recognised. This was Harold Godwinson, a man who must not be crossed. I felt sure that Sweyn's life was in danger.

- *And what of Hakon? What of the boy? He has become as another son to us.*

- *Hakon will remain here, under our protection.*

HAROLD GODWINSON - THE LAST SAXON

And with that Harold was gone. Godwin had summoned him to Winchester, where the Earl was to throw a banquet in the king's honour, and Harold and Tostig were summoned to attend.

- The king wants us all present. There will be oaths to be renewed. It is all part of his revenge.

If I had known that this was the last time I would see Godwin, I might have been softer with him on our parting. As it was, I told him that I wanted the boys to spend more time with their father. In the last three years he had become a stranger to them and to me.

- This is what it is to marry into an earl's family, Edith. You must make sacrifices, as your mother-in-law has done.

The word marriage was spoken without irony. I had hoped that I could persuade Harold to finally seal our vows in a Christian ceremony.

- I make sacrifices willingly, Godwin. But the boys need their father.

- What your boys need, Edith, is the certainty that their father has a place at the king's side. The place I have carved out as my own, will one day be his. If he is not there, others will fill the void and all my actions, everything I have done to raise the House of Godwin will be for nothing. The Earls of Wessex will cease to wield power and influence in the land. Then where will your children be, Edith?

News of Sweyn's death reached us by letter.

From what we can gather, Earl Sweyn, died somewhere on his return from Jerusalem. The details are not clear. One of his fellows says he died in Constantinople; another that it was at Lycia that he met his end. Some say that he was killed by Saracens; others that he was murdered in the night by a Saxon soldier, who disappeared at the same time. Whatever the truth, Sweyn has met a noble end and his sins will be forgiven by God for he has made the ultimate sacrifice; death on a pilgrimage to the Holy Land. What more could God or man ask of him?

So Sweyn was dead. Harold was rid of him. He was now his father's heir and Sweyn would no longer embarrass the family name. The story of the Saxon soldier rang true. Harold had a long reach. And he was ruthless in matters of power.

And when Godwin himself died suddenly – a fit or seizure I was told – I began to suspect my husband's hand was behind it all. I had no proof. Of course, there was no proof. No-one could forgive patricide, but two deaths of such significance in so short a space of time makes one suspicious. That's all I am saying. I held my boys tighter. Who was next? Surely, they were safe from their father? It was Harold himself who told me.

- It was Easter Monday, he was alone with the king, breaking their fast together. Suddenly he was lying at the king's feet, bereft of speech, unable to move. He was carried to Edward's private chamber. Three days he lay there, until he finally passed away. It smacks of poison, Edith, and poison is a woman's weapon. There is no proof, of course, but I would look no further than Emma, the king's mother. She had her reasons to hate our father. Our father has been murdered, of that I'm certain.

I too was sure of it. Though Emma was not my chief suspect. Yes, she had her reasons for wanting him dead. It was at Godwin's door she lay the butchering of her son Alfred. But why wait so long? There were others who would benefit from Godwin's demise. Not least Harold Godwinson.

Godwin was buried with full honours at Winchester, the greatest of the earls who had borne the title Wessex. Kingmaker and father to the Saxon people. There was a new Earl, a new father. Without Sweyn to succeed him, it was Harold who assumed land and titles. One third of England was ours; its land, its people and its wealth. There was talk too that Tostig would reclaim the titles and land lost in banishment. Siward, Earl of Northumbria was an old man – a Viking by birth and sympathy. Tostig would become the new Earl, on his death. Tostig, with Harold's help, would ensure that he was not left waiting too long. Soon all of England would be Saxon. Soon all of England would pay allegiance to the House of Godwin. And the old patriarch had been right. Our children's place was assured, their inheritance safe.

But still there were enemies all about us. As the Godwinson star rose, others, living in their long shadows grew jealous and fearful. Months after the death of Siward, Hakon went missing. My boys treated Hakon as a brother; they had known him almost from his birth, and while they knew he was a cousin, and a bastard boy at that, they loved him as they loved their brothers. It was a cold morning in December. Snow had been threatening for a week before it finally arrived, covering the green fields and the bare, black trees. It dampened the sound of footsteps. The boys loved it: Godwin, Edmund and Magnus took out a sled, crudely crafted by their father and took it in turns to haul it up to the top of Senlac Hill before hurling down. I watched them, not feeling the cold wind, warmed by their shouts of joy.

- *Where's Hakon? Why isn't he here with you? He loves the snow.*

Godwin left the younger boys to their game and came to where I stood. His hands were red and raw. I rubbed them in mine to bring the blood up.

- *Asleep, mother. Hakon didn't answer when we called. And we didn't want to wait for him. The snow was too inviting.*

I smiled at him.

- *Well, I'm sure he is awake now. Fetch him out into the snow. Give him a turn on the sled.*

I watched him trudge through the snow, more than a little reluctant to leave his younger brothers having all the fun. I watched him enter the house and then a few minutes later he returned, still alone.

- *Perhaps he sneaked out while I was looking for him.*

But Hakon was nowhere to be seen. It was one of the servant girls who told me.

- *Two men came for him mistress. They told me you had sent them. I said I would go and talk to you first, but they assured me you knew, that you had sent for him. Hakon himself seemed calm enough.*

Someone had taken the boy. But why? Perhaps it was the mother's people. Perhaps they wanted him to return to Flanders. But they would not have come like thieves in the night. I summoned Harold back from Winchester, where he was on his hundred circuit, where he dispensed justice. He came at the end of the day.

- *This is no maternal snatch, Edith. They mean to hold the boy hostage for some reason or other.*

- *But who has him?*

HAROLD GODWINSON - THE LAST SAXON

I was fearful for Hakon. He was a quiet, reserved boy who even at the age of ten, was slight and could not defend himself.

- *I will find out, Edith. They will not get away with it. Hakon's disappearance is an attempt to threaten me. But they have miscalculated, whoever it is. I will not be cowed by the kidnapping of my brother's son.*

I swore to never let the boys out of my sight; so long as they were young enough to be in my care, I would not let them go; it was my duty to keep them safe. I had let Hakon down, and I must not let these men take our boys. As a gesture against Harold, it was pointless. Harold cared for Hakon for his father's sake, but he was not one of his own. But I felt differently. He had been in my charge, and I had let him down. I had let bad men come in the night to take him to… take him to God knows where.

- *Edith, be certain, I shall find out where he is, and who is responsible for this.*

There was no more talk of marriage. Harold deemed it unnecessary. We lived as husband and wife, and he saw no reason to change the arrangement. I found it strongly ironic that he, Harold of Wessex, who opposed all things Viking, would nevertheless be content with a Danish-style marriage. But Harold is a man of convenient contradiction, a politician. He met regularly with the Witan, the wise men who carried out much of the day-to-day business of running the country, and who were closest advisers of the king. Harold wanted to be sure that their counsel was wise, and that it suited his own position. He came to see us in Senlac a few weeks after Hakon's disappearance.

- *She has him,* he announced.
- *The boy's mother?*
- *The king's mother, the Norman whore!*
- *Emma? Why does she have our boy?*

Harold gave me that look. The one that says hold your tongue. He was not "our boy" as he constantly reminded me.

- *She has taken him to Normandy?*
- *To Normandy? Why?*
- *She thinks that to have an heir of Godwin in her grasp will make it easier for Duke William when he becomes king.*
- *Will the king name William as his heir?*
- *He is Edward's cousin. And our king has no natural heirs. Who is to say that Emma will not persuade him? Perhaps she has done so already.*
- *And what is Hakon's part in all this?*
- *Hakon will become Earl of Wessex, if William becomes king. They will rekindle the idea of his being descended from Cnut himself. It is a clever move.*
- *And what of the boy? Is he well?*
- *Emma tells me he is being well treated, that her Norman kin are civilised and know how to treat noble sons.*
- *Is he lost then? Forever?*
- *Not forever, Edith. When it is expedient to do so, I shall make the journey to this bastard Duke to claim back the bastard boy.*

The words were deliberately chosen, to hurt me. Were our children not equally illegitimate in the eyes of the church? But there was no arguing with Harold Godwinson. He returned to Winchester the next day to the court sittings. That was the end of it.

Godwin's legacy lives on. The ruthless march to power continues even after his death. Harold is his father's son. Earl Harold of Wessex had grown even more powerful than his father. And I suspected that Earl of Wessex would never be enough. Harold had higher ambitions.

Confessor

HAROLD GODWINSON - THE LAST SAXON

WIFE

Of all men, it was Godwin I hated most; and of all men, I feared him most. It may not have been his hand that blinded and butchered my brother, Alfred, but the Earl of Wessex was certainly responsible. It was not for nothing he was known as The Kingmaker; he had certainly placed me upon the throne. And I didn't doubt he would do his best to remove me if I failed to pay the price. My poorly-advised father had never solved the problem of the Vikings. It was his blind eyes to the extortion of Danegeld that led to his downfall. And it was Godwin who had been the chief architect of his decline. Ethelred's saving grace, and the only reason he had been tolerated at all, had been that he was from the House of Wessex. And that has been my salvation too. But it was not my father that gained me the throne, it was Godwin, working in league with my mother, Queen Emma. I had assumed that the office of king was the highest in the land, but England is a strange place. Here the king rules only by the will of the earls. And the chief of these was Godwin. I had spent twenty-five of my years in exile. It was not a time I remember with any happiness. My mother had sworn to put me on the throne, but her early attempts came to nothing, and Godwin had killed brother Alfred, and would have done the same to me, had I not escaped back into exile.

I grew up in Normandy. It was pleasant enough, but I spent too many hours staring across the water that kept me from what my mother always called my true inheritance.

- *You are the son of a king, and the brother of a king.* It was true enough, though to be more accurate Harthacnut was my half-brother, and my mother had held little affection for him when he was alive. Those early days of solitude made me the man I am now, preferring the company of books to the company of men, especially when so few men could be trusted. It was Robert of Jumièges that showed me the true path. Reading was my first love, and the illustrated bibles he sent to me from the Norman abbeys were my dearest companions.

- A king must know more than what he can read, Edward, my mother was fond of saying.

- But a king must know by what divine right he rules. If I am to be king, God will lead me to the throne.

- If you are to be king you will need a sword as well as a book, Edward. The coronation in London preceded my fortieth birthday by a year. St Paul's was a fine setting, but I determined to move the court, and make a new palace at Westminster, a new cathedral, built to the glory of God, on the sight of the small church further west along the river, A new cathedral for a new age,

It seemed sound politics to marry Godwin's daughter, Edith of Wessex. The only way to hold on to power is to keep enemies close, and what could be closer than to have Godwin as my father-in-law. Surely this marriage would put an end to the threat he posed. I had decided, even before my marriage that I would eschew fatherhood. Our marriage is still not consummated. I had no desire to lay alongside Edith, as beautiful as she was. She was a queen, but she was also Godwin's daughter. Besides, I had determined that my body was for God's work and through abstinence would come my martyrdom. By then I had been on the throne for three years and the early fears of being deposed - blinded and beheaded too - were fading. The marriage to Edith would bring me security, especially as I had agreed to have her crowned alongside me – a rare enough event in these days. Bit by bit, Godwin secured vast areas of land for himself and his sons. And of all the sons, it was Harold that I feared most. His father had learned to bend with the wind. But Harold was more obdurate, more stubborn. The only thing in my favour with Harold Godwinson was that I would never have an heir. The marriage to Edith had been a move by Godwin to create a place for his family to become regents, kin of the queen, uncles of the princes. But when they saw that I had no intention of letting that happen, I felt sure they set even greater office in their sights. I could never have a child with Edith. It would give them what they wanted most. A king from the house of Godwin.

I sent them away, exiled them, Edith too. Their actions have brought this upon themselves. Again, the rumours abound of Sweyn's connections to Cnut. And I am under pressure from others, especially my Norman kin, to keep a check on these rebellious earls, who mean to take my power from me, even if they cannot take the throne. And how right I have been proved. Harold, returning from Wales, raised an army against us. I have allowed them to return. The power they wield will break me otherwise. But Sweyn must stay in exile. Perhaps his pilgrimage will bring him to repentance.

When Godwin died, I hoped some of the danger would pass with him. I know they blamed me – or perhaps my mother. He was poisoned, I am told. The old man had a fit, there before me, writhing in agonies upon the floor. I know I should be sorry that the old man is dead, but in truth I feel a sense of relief. Despite what we are told about revenge being the Lord's, I cannot help but remember that this old man was responsible for the cruel death of my brother Alfred. And for that alone he will not enter Heaven. Harold Godwinson, in the absence of Sweyn has assumed the title of Earl of Wessex and has pledged his allegiance. His oaths are worth nothing, but for now there is peace.

I went to see Edith at Wilton Abbey. She is the queen and I pay her the reverence she is due. I mean to bring her out of exile, back to Westminster.

- *How is my queen?*
- *Well, husband? How is my lord?*
- *Your father's death must have been hard for you to bear.*
- *He was a great man, King Edward.*
- *A great man with many faults.*
- *We are all sinners my lord; from the serf to the king himself. We are made sinners by Adam's fall.*
- *Indeed we are, Edith.*
- *And what of Harold, your brother? How does he wear his new clothes?*
- *Harold was born to be Earl of Wessex. Sweyn's actions over the years have taken such rights away from him, despite his natural birthright.*
- *And should I fear him, Edith, this Harold Godwinson.*
- *It is a king's lot to fear all men, Edward. I know he sends his wife to spy on me. He seeks ways to be closer to Your Majesty.*
- *And what of you? Do you miss my company?*
- *I am a queen, and do not have the same rights to choose as others do, Edward. I married you, expecting to bring you heirs, but you have forsworn my bed and now I am sent away to a nunnery to live out my days.*

HAROLD GODWINSON - THE LAST SAXON

- *It is my pact with God, Edith. I have made my body a temple to the Lord. I know it brings you pain.*
- *It would be easier to bear if I could be closer to you.*

I suspected her double-meaning was deliberate.

- *I have decided. Now that I have allowed your family to return, I want you to take your place again, beside me. I miss your wisdom as well as your guiding hands.*
- *I am to return home?*
- *Yes, Edith. Home to Westminster.*

I left her to gather her belongings and she returned to the palace. I had missed her. Edith is a good – and loyal - wife, and a good wife is much to be valued, especially when she is loyal. So often she shows the wisdom I first saw in her. There is work for her to do by my side. Not least she will give me the security I seek and peace for England. I hear what is said of her: she is a hard woman; though she stands modestly behind me, her will is strong and her temper ill. They are right. She is, in all ways, her father's daughter. But she adorns the palace, not just in herself but with the works she commissions for us. She is an asset to a King of England, and in truth, I have missed her. She is a pious woman, but Edith is not content with storing up treasure in Heaven alone. I am not blind to her faults, but all of us have them.

- *My brother has been to see me, Edward.*
- *Harold?*
- *Tostig. He has asked for recognition of his name.*

HAROLD GODWINSON - THE LAST SAXON

- What is it he wants, Edith?

- Northumbria.

I had suspected this. Not satisfied with Wessex, the Godwinsons wanted to acquire the whole of England. Northumbria was highly prized, and it was strategically important in order to keep the Vikings at arm's length. Tostig would antagonise them.

- There is already an Earl of Northumbria.

- It is true, Edward. Earl Siward holds the titles, but he is not a Saxon. He is a Viking by nature as well as by birth. He will not support you if the Danes come.

- I will not take his titles from him, Edith. To place a Saxon Earl in charge would incite them. It would invite an invasion, and England has fought enough wars. Earl Siward was Cnut's man, and his people respect him. Siward fought for our name in Scotland. He defeated the usurper Macbeth and restored the exiled Malcolm, and with him, brought peace to our neighbours. While they are at peace, while they are in England's debt, I shall sleep more easily. No; Siward is a loyal earl, and I will not strip him of the titles he bears so well.

- He is an old man, Edward. And old men die.

Edith was right. He was an old man, and it wasn't long before his death caused stirrings. Rumours of a Danish fleet were brought to me. It was Edith herself who carried the news. And I wondered if she had played a part in the old man's death.

- Only Tostig can hold Northumbria, Edward. He is your kin. He is loyal, and he knows how to deal with rebellious earls.

Some may have thought me weak, but Edith was right. Whatever my feelings for the Godwinsons, they were Saxons, and they were committed to keeping this Saxon king firmly on his throne. Tostig was invited to York, and I greeted him there with the title of Earl of

Northumbria. I was aware of the resentment in this city. Tostig would have to overcome these resentments, and while he was busy securing his own position, he would have little time to threaten us.

They have it all now, these Wessexes. Their reach stretches from the Southern coast to the borders of Scotland, and from Wales to the Wash. But I remind them that they hold it for their king. England is a Saxon country now. There is no doubting my queen's influence and power, but I can as easily remove it from her, so while it benefits me, while it helps keep this kingdom safe, I am content.

I know that Harold and Tostig are uneasy together. They are brothers but each resents the other's power. I think Tostig still harbours a grudge against Harold for the part he played in Sweyn's exile; but for Harold, Sweyn would still be here, in England, assuming the titles of his dead father. Tostig said as much to Edith, and she was happy to report it to me.

- *They are my brothers, Edward, but while they fight amongst themselves, they do us no harm. Their rivalry will help keep the kingdom in balance.*

This was her wisdom. This was her value.

Edith has the ear of the Witan too. They are my wise men. They give me counsel and I am stronger for their wisdom. But I know that the queen is highly regarded by them, and she offers her opinions in matters of dispute. I have my sources, just as she does. Most of all, I have my mother. It is Queen Emma who keeps Edith in check, with her spies in the court, and it is Edith who holds back my mother's ambitions for her cousins in Normandy. All is in balance. Precarious, yes, but balanced. My mother had returned to Normandy some years ago. Been returned, reluctantly. *I am ill, and close to death*, she told me. *I want to see my son before I die.* She has sent for me. *When a mother commands, even a king quakes* was her favourite saying. And while quaking didn't actually describe my feelings, I knew that there was as much peril from the narrow channel as from the northern seas. While the new Earl of Northumbria took care of the Danish threat, I needed to keep the Normans at arm's length. Visits to Normandy were less frequent but were still common enough. Harold advised me against the trip. But he knew that I would go.

- *While you are there, ask after Hakon. Secure his release.*
- *Hakon is not a prisoner, Harold. He is my mother's guest. She brings him up as one of her own grandchildren.*
- *Hakon belongs here. Queen Emma keeps him for a time when he can be useful to her?*
- *We shall ask after the boy, make sure he is well. He is dear to Queen Edith's heart. He is her nephew; her eldest brother's orphan child. I shall see no harm comes to him. I am the boy's king. Trust me in this matter, Harold.*
- *I would trust you more if the boy were not held in a Norman stronghold, by a Norman queen.*
- *Let it be, Harold. I shall seek him out. I shall talk to the boy. Trust me in this.*

Edith would remain behind. With Harold's backing, England was in good hands. Edith revelled in taking the reins. She was an excellent horsewoman, and she was just as sure with the reigns of the kingdom as she was in the saddle of a horse. Edith may never be a mother of kings, but she was the mother of England, and I trusted her. My mother saw her as *just another Godwin spawn*. She was convinced that on my return I would be greeted with rebellion.

- Edith has her father's temperament, and her brother's iron will. You should not leave the kingdom in her hands.

- Then, mother, I must stay in England, and our Norman kindred must do without Edward.

Edith and I travelled down to Senlac together and early the next morning I stepped aboard the ship that would carry me to Normandy. The sea was narrow but treacherous, and I was not a good sailor, despite my Danish roots. It was a relief to see the river open up and the port of Westerham appear. Once in the sheltered harbour it was a safe journey along the river to Caen. It still felt like a homecoming, after all these years away. And knowing Queen Emma would be there to greet me would make it more so.

HAROLD GODWINSON - THE LAST SAXON

JOUSTING

A storm delayed us. Even before my feet touched Norman soil, I knew exactly the purpose of my journey. This was much more than a family reunion; it was to be a discussion on succession. Queen Emma, restored again to her position of power and influence, held sway in Normandy, but now that she was ill, close to death, her influence was no longer going to help me. I came to William's fortress, where Queen Emma lay in state. The storm had held us up; I arrived too late. I was allowed to sit with her body, and I admit to crying real tears. She had done much to deserve my anger and hatred but I knew, that without her influence and power, my rule in England would never have come to pass. I sat with her, talked to her body and told her of my fears. But, unlike in the past, she gave no answer, no advice. She stayed silent.

After the funeral, I was anxious to return. William summoned me, smiled and turned his hands together in an unctuous manner. He took a moment to frame his words. Such was his nature. He and I had spent some years together as boys and young men and I knew how he prepared for momentous words. He controlled the stammer that would often mar his speech.

- *I mourn the death of your mother, King Edward. She was a great queen, who ruled over three lands. She was a great Norman too.*
- *Thank you, Duke William.*

William of Normandy had fought hard for his title and would not expect me to address him in any other way. To him I was always King Edward, and he expected me to use his title in return for mine. But he was also a close kinsman. So our speeches were mixed with kinship and kingship

HAROLD GODWINSON - THE LAST SAXON

- *I regret your lack of heirs…*
- *It is a choice I have made, cousin.*
- *But it is one that leaves your England exposed.*
- *Exposed, Duke William?*
- *To rebellious Saxon earls.*
- *They will not oppose me, cousin.*
- *Not while you are alive.*
- *You have a solution, I suspect.*
- *Make the succession clear. Through your mother, I am your closest kin. She made it plain to me, before she died, that England should be mine… when you go to join her.*
- *My position has always been clear. In England it is The Witan that rules on such matters.*
- *But the Witan needs to know its king's mind, King Edward.*
- *And so it shall, Duke William.*

We were playing now, this duke and I. He took his time before he finally got to the point.

- *They need to know that your wish is to see that I, William Duke of Normandy, is your chosen heir.*
- *There will be opposition.*
- *From Godwinson, no doubt. He is the queen's brother; is that his only claim?*
- *He is a Saxon, cousin, and the Witan…*
- *The Witan will follow its king's wishes in this respect. So, cousin,* and his use of the word made it sound very menacing, *what will the king propose about his succession?*

There was movement in the room, a sudden stiffening to attention as the men behind me moved their hands to their swords. This was not a request. My cousin saw it as his God-given right. William had always been concerned for his birthright. He was a bastard son, and many had already challenged by force of arms his right to be Duke of Normandy. But here he was, still holding the title, and holding the King of England too.

- *You should know, Duke William, that the matter was settled some years ago. The English earls are not to be trusted. If one of them becomes king, others will fight to take it from him. There will be war and England will divide, as it has done so many times. This is not the legacy I seek. Queen Emma made you a promise after she spoke with me. You are already named as heir. You have no need for these men who surround me, armed and ready. Had you intended to hold me here?*

There was the usual long pause before Duke William spoke again. There was even a trace of a smile on his lips. A rare sight indeed. Instead of answering my question...

- *Then you must make your wishes clear to the Witan. I want no doubt.*

- *There will be none, cousin.*

He turned on his heel, and the guards around him followed him out. As quickly as that I was alone. The journey home left me much to ponder. Announcing William as my true heir would be poorly received by Harold Godwinson.

The new church at Westminster was taking shape. St Peter's monastery had long-since fallen into disrepair. There were only a few monks now in residence; it was a poor place and unworthy of holy worship. Westminster Palace was already the home of the court and the new abbey, under my leadership, would become the centre of English worship. I visit it as often as I can, talking through the plans with masons and churchwrights. It was to be built in the new style, borrowed from the grand cathedrals I had seen in Normandy. And it was in this great edifice that I would be buried. Winchester would lose its prominence; it was too closely aligned to the Wessex clan, and the change would show them who was in charge. It would also be an act of piety. A grand work to the glory of God.

Weeks after my return, Harold requested an audience. I granted him access and he came with many of his followers, carrying swords.

- *Your men will not be allowed to enter with you. You have nothing to fear here at the court, Harold.*

- *My father died here, King Edward. And some say it was a suspicious death.*

- *Your father was an old man. In any case there are as many rumours about you plotting his death as there are that claim we were responsible.*

- *Nevertheless, I have cause to be wary.*

- *Not here in this place, Harold Godwinson. If you wish to talk with your king, you will do it unarmed. For we recall our brother's death and the memory of it still pains us.*

It was yet another joust between us, and as had always to be the case, the king won. The men withdrew, taking their swords with them.

- *You are newly returned from Normandy, King Edward.*

- *We desired to see our mother one last time before she died. And to bring her body home to be interred at Winchester. The Duke wanted* us to leave the body there in Normandy. We determined otherwise. Unfortunately, the storms delayed us.

- *God determined it, then?*
- *If the storm is God's handiwork, then yes, it would be fair to say that.* Queen Emma's last words were not shared with us.
- *I have heard that you have spoken to the bastard William in Normandy.*
- *He and I are cousins, Harold. Closer kin than even you and I. And we were together for Queen Emma's funeral. It would be strange if we had not spoken.*

The Earl of Wessex waved his hand, as though swatting away the point.

- *Promises were made; oaths taken.*
- *Were they?*
- *About the succession.*
- *We let our cousin know that it is the Witan that rules on such matters.*
- *Their ruling would be unnecessary if you had a true heir. A son.*
- *A nephew for you to groom and prepare? Is that your meaning?*
- *A son would settle the matter.*
- *There will be no son, Harold Godwinson. We are sworn to celibacy and an oath to God is not taken lightly.*
- *And the Norman bastard knows this.*
- *He is well-informed as are you by all accounts.*
- *And is he so named?*
- *William of Normandy is our closest kin. He has the right to make his claim before the Witan.*
- *And what guidance will the king give his ministers?*

- They know William's position. What will the Earl of Wessex do to show he respects the Witan's wisdom? How will he show his loyalty to his king?

We were jousting again. Our lances were poised ready, the horses scraped their hooves, anxious to be in combat. The two combatants continued to talk as though they were speaking of others.

- The Earl of Wessex will abide by the decision of the Witan as he has always done.

It was over. The king had won.

- We are delighted to hear it. Your loyalty does you credit, Harold. Meanwhile there is work to be done for a loyal earl. The Welsh prince must be taught a lesson. He cannot cross our borders and ransack English villages. Bring us that prince's head. We will have it adorning the high tower at Hereford cathedral. It will make a fine topping for the new towers we have had built there.

Harold thought for a moment before replying.

- And who better than Leofric, your Earl of Mercia, to teach the Welsh a lesson.

- Will you join him?

- Not at this time, King Edward. Leofric and my father were sworn enemies, but they refused to fight each other even as you had requested, to avoid the cost of so many Saxon lives. It would antagonise the earl if we suggest he cannot do this without our help. He can count on us if things do not go well. As can your majesty.

With a stiff, formal nod of his head, Harold Godwinson left the palace.

HAROLD GODWINSON - THE LAST SAXON

Leofric dealt with the rebels, driving them back across the Marches. Ryhdderch's head was hung atop of the tower at Hereford and tribute was brought to compensate for the sacked villages and the English lives lost. The death of one Welsh chieftain, does not end the conflict, however. They are like the hydra; as we cut off one head, more appear and each bears arms against us. I must send more troops to the borders. The Earl of Mercia will once again lead them with his double-headed eagle banner.

I do not know what to make of Leofric. He is a Saxon earl who swears loyalty to me, but he will not take up arms against my enemies, even when they are his enemies. I suspect he is like Harold Godwinson: Saxon first and English second. I have tested him often and he has shown himself to be our supporter. At Worcester, in the early years of my rule, he punished them for killing the tax inspectors. I know how hard that must have been for him. Worcester was his spiritual home, from where his people came. I have called him to Westminster and now he stands before me. Harold Godwinson attends too. I think it best to have the two of them together for this.

- Leofric. You are most welcome. We think of you and the Earl of Wessex here as the most loyal of all my earls. I was like a father who tells each son that he is their favourite. *But word has come to me that your son has plotted against me.*

Leofric, a bear of a man, stood tall in front of me.

- Aelfgar is no traitor, King Edward. It is rumour and gossip that paint him to be so.

- And from where do these rumours originate, Leofric?

- I suspect they come out of Wessex, King Harold.

Harold Godwinson stepped forward.

- We should not be surprised, Your Majesty, if Mercia is unable to control his son. If the stories are to be believed, he has no control over his wife either.

Leofric turned towards Harold. His hand went to his belt, but their swords had been taken from them both before they were allowed in their king's presence. Harold continued to taunt Leofric.

- The Lady Godiva rode naked through the streets in protest against your majesty's legitimate call to raise taxes.

- It is not so, King Edward. It is not so. It is true she gave ear to the complaints of our villagers, who struggle to pay their rents and the extra tax we levy at your behest. But she has never ridden naked through the streets of Coventry. It is a lie, to ridicule me and my family.

Earl against earl; this is how to keep my kingdom in balance. I held my hands up. They turned to me.

- Your son – perhaps at your wife's command - has made it known that these taxes are not to be paid. This is treason, Leofric. We could have him captured and put to death.

It was an idle threat, and I suspect Leofric knew it.

- He is no traitor. If there are disloyal earls here in England perhaps you should look no further than Wessex.

Once again the two men faced each other, hands instinctively drawn to their empty scabbards.

- But we shall spare his life, Leofric. As a mark of our love for you. But Aelfgar will have his titles taken from him. He must leave England.

- Where will he go? Where will my son live?

- Let him go across the water – to Ireland perhaps. They are good Christians there and he can do penance.

Leofric exploded, his anger no longer able to be contained.

HAROLD GODWINSON - THE LAST SAXON

- You would send him away, stripped of rank and titles, for no crime?

- We have given judgement, Leofric. Make sure he understands. Go and tell him what we have said. He is not beyond redemption, Leofric. No man is beyond forgiveness.

Leofric gave a look at Godwinson which would have frozen the blood of a lesser man, and turned on his heels. The noise of his stamping footsteps echoed after him. Harold waited until the room was silent again.

- And what will happen to Aelfgar's lands and titles, Edward? Who is to manage them in his absence?

It was a year later that Harold stood here at Westminster and told me what I already knew.

- You are too lenient with your enemies, Edward.

- Should a king not show mercy, as God shows mercy?

- Aelfgar has raised an army. Were he already dead, this could have been avoided.

- I spared your brother Sweyn many times. Should I not have spared his life?

I heard his silence and smiled.

- Our reign is one of mercy. I am Edward, King by God's grace.

- You are wise Edward, and merciful, but mercy must not be seen as weakness. Traitorous Mercia will use it against you. This army, of Irish and Welsh forces have crossed the border. He has joined forces with Llewellyn and together they have taken Hereford and use it as a stronghold against your majesty.

HAROLD GODWINSON - THE LAST SAXON

It was true. I had heard it already.

- *Then what should we do, Wessex? Wars will bankrupt us. Wars will result in the death of English men and women, then will lead to more rebellions when we have to raise more taxes to pay for them. Peace is what we seek.*

- *I will lead your armies to Hereford and drive the rebels back into Wales. Once they are back across the borders, you should sue for peace.*

And so it was. Harold Godwinson gathered men from every quarter of his vast lands and raised an army. They recaptured Hereford, but this time there were no heads mounted. And he acted as my emissary. Aelfgar was allowed to return and when Leofric died, an old man disappointed by life, his son took on the rank and title of his father. Siward, Godwin and now Leofric, the last of the great Saxon Earls were dead. They had been thorns in my side throughout my reign. With their deaths, I should have felt some safety, some peace. But the next generation were even more ambitious than their fathers. And most ambitious of all was Harold Godwinson.

HAROLD GODWINSON - THE LAST SAXON

HUNTING

If being King of England was my lot, then hunting was my pleasure. I felt more that I had been put on earth to ride and hunt, than to be royal. It took me away from the rigours of politics, a world of intrigue and lies; and it took me to the wild and free pleasures of riding – without a crown to constrain my mind. The kill was incidental. I no longer ate meat every day, and I ate only fish on Fridays as the Lord had taught us. Sundays were fast days, holy, spent in the company of priests and bishops. It was the hunting that sustained me; that and the knowledge that I was doing God's work. The deer were worthy foe, and we rarely caught sight of them in the herds that seemed to fill the royal parks – except when we sought them out. How did they know we were there? They were God's creatures and by His grace most survived our expeditions.

William in Normandy was licking his garlicky lips at the thought of, one day, succeeding here. He had secured my mother's promise before her death, and waited only for me to confirm his right of succession. I had stalled him but he still licked those greasy lips of his. From Norway there were rumours that Harald, known to his allies as well as his foes as "the hard ruler", had set his eyes on England. He was still too occupied with his own battles with Denmark, but the time would come when he too would make a bid, by force of arms most probably. Here, in England, other types of hunting were taking place. Harold, Earl of Wessex was expanding his power. The other earls now looked on with envy – and some concern - at his expanding empire, not least his brother Tostig who wants more titles, more land. After the Battle of Hereford, Harold had assumed the title Earl of Hereford and has made his opposition to a Norman succession clear to all who will listen. Neither could the Witan be trusted. They were no less corruptible than the earls. Balancing these rivals was more difficult even than catching the elusive deer, and infinitely less pleasurable. I am weary of the day-to-day political intrigue.

Apart from hunting deer, I am determined to chase after veneration. For centuries after my death I shall be known as a saint; a king who, every day, embodies God's spirit and grace. I am not built for martyrdom. Pain frightens me, but there are other ways to reach such a goal. So now my life is simple. Church in the early hours, hunting in the day and then a light repast, rarely of meat, before returning to my prayers. Add to that the regular inspection of my new Abbey of Saint Peter at Westminster, which grows grander day by day, and which will be a fitting monument to God and his anointed King. Is that not truly the life of a saint?

- I seek the king's permission, and his blessing.
- To marry your daughter to a Welsh rebel? To a man who killed your own uncle? What does your daughter say to the proposal?
- Ealdgyth is an obedient daughter. She sees the marriage as a way to bring peace to the kingdom. Llewellyn will make her a fine husband.
- We had thought that both she and you had set your sights on Harold as husband to your daughter.
- Wessex is not free to marry.
- Wessex has no wife in the sight of God. You will know that he and Edith were handfasted.

HAROLD GODWINSON - THE LAST SAXON

- Harold seeks no second wife. The Welsh prince will bring his own advantage to our family and greater safety to you, Edward.

- And what of Llewellyn? Has he not taken a wife? Is she not still living?

- A woman married by conquest is easily set aside, King Edward.

Aelfgar knelt before me. He was his father's son all right. Obsequious when it suited, as it did now. Just as Leofric had been – his father's son. It is a pity he inherited none of his mother's courage.   Godiva had been bold enough to ride through Coventry – naked I am assured. How petty it all seems. Why could they not use their king as example? I have chosen my wife, and will certainly not marry again. Daughters are seen as chattels by these earls; possessions to be bartered for land and power. I see that look on the poor girl's face. She will not make a willing bride. But if it will bring peace from over the marches.

- And this union will bring us peace?

- And prosperity, your majesty.

His prosperity I assumed!

- Then so be it. You have my blessing.

And Aelfgar left the court, taking his poor daughter with him. And the Earl of Mercia was right. The raids ceased. Whether this was brought about by Ealdgyth's marriage or by the build-up of forces by Harold at Hereford is unclear.   Each of the earls, Wessex and Mercia assured me that their strategy was the reason for peace. I care not which of them is responsible if it gives me time for my beloved hunting. There were stories of Llewellyn's battles along the border, capturing all the territory that ran along his side of The Great Dyke. And he became King of Wales. My equal! The real winner in all this was Aelfgar. Harold was less than happy with developments, but keeping Mercia and Wessex in equilibrium served me well. Equilibrium is good for hunting.

After fifteen years of my reign, England seems a more settled place. The country matches my own progress. As a young man, I had been troubled, easily swayed, turning this way and that, just as England had been. But I was God's man now, and England's was a godly land. He, in return brought me peace. Not without a price; not without the occasional worry; not without a fear of death. But peace. What disturbances there were came chiefly from Wessex. Godwin's fourth son, Leofwine, was given titles and land carved out from Harold's territories in the south and east, and in return laid claim to more of the land that had once belonged to Leofric's son in East Anglia. So while my hunting took up much of my time the Godwinsons also hunted with some success. Harold and his brothers grew ever more powerful; but Wales and Scotland respected our borders. Their kings confined their hunting to their own kingdoms.

- *Llewellyn is no respecter of England and its king, Edward. He must be taught a lesson.*

Harold was at the court. I had planned a visit to Westminster. My great church is almost complete.

- *Mercia assured me that Llewellyn was no threat to us.*

- *While he rules the borders, the Welsh king is a focus for rebels who would bring us a Norman duke, or a Norwegian king.*

- *His daughter's marriage…*

HAROLD GODWINSON - THE LAST SAXON

- We should not trust our daughters to bring us the peace that war alone can guarantee.

This sounded like his father's words. When I had married Harold's sister, Godwin saw it as to his advantage, but it never held him back from voicing opposition to me.

- Can you not deal with this in other ways? Are there not peace treaties that can be forged? Are we to lose more Saxon men?

- Their sacrifice will keep the enemy locked outside our gates. We need to show them that there are no allies to support an invasion of England.

- So be it, Harold. So be it.

And I watched him go. It seems that Harold Godwinson is a better hunter than me. He has greater success. But I know where his true aim is. He hunts for succession. He hunts for kingship. He hunts for my word to the Witan. Harold of Wessex, William of Normandy and Harald of Norway. They all have their eyes on England.

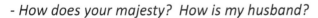

- How does your majesty? How is my husband?

Edith has accompanied me to Westminster. She marvels at the work of the master-masons, letting her hands wander over the smooth stone walls. The bright summer sunshine has warmed the stones and given them a special golden colour. God can see how fine a church we build here for Him.

- And when will it be finished, Edward?

- In time for my interment, Edith. It will house my bones. And all will come, from near and far to worship at this shrine.

HAROLD GODWINSON - THE LAST SAXON

- And what of my bones, Edward?

- They will lay next to mine. You are Queen Edith and you will be revered.

- Not in Winchester then with my ancestors?

- Winchester is a Wessex shrine. You have overleaped that title. As Queen of England, you shall lie here next to me. We shall be together forever, just as we swore at our wedding?

- It is a pity then that we shall have no children to mourn us, and to follow us to St Peter's.

- Our people are our children, Edith. They shall mourn us; they shall pay homage to our bones.

- And what of your successors?

I knew we would come to it. Edith is Queen but she is also Wessex. She seeks to know my mind on the succession.

- Look at me, Edith. Does your husband – your King – does he look to you as if he is about to die?

She takes my hand in hers. Whatever else is true of Edith, I know she loves me.

- My lord is well. He is hale and hearty. All this hunting brings colour to his cheeks...

I take her meaning for I know my face is pale.

- ... and strength to his sinews. Of course King Edward will live a long life...

I hear a *but* coming and here it is.

- ... but without a successor named there is uncertainty about the future of England.

- You can tell your brother that England is a Saxon kingdom and it will remain so. I am from the Wessex line, his line, your line. I will not fail in my duty to England.

HAROLD GODWINSON - THE LAST SAXON

And there it ends, for the master-masons want to show me their progress with the altar. Edith mounts her horse again and returns to the palace. I have no doubt that, once there, she will convey the news to her brother. And he will be satisfied. For now.

I feel the horse beneath me, its power and strength. I am one with him as we fly across the parkland in hot pursuit. I am at the head of the group; those in the hunting party make sure of it. If there is to be a kill, it is the King's. Boaz – the swift – runs against the wind, making light of his power, leading the others on. It is a good name for a horse. Like his namesake in the bible, Boaz is my kinsman-redeemer. I am the weaker of us, in need of his strength, and he knows it, this Boaz. He carries me safely across hedge and ditch and, at last, to the heart of the herd. He stands still, catching a breath, eye-to-eye with the Great Stag with his twelve points. He is the Royal Stag, fit to be hunted by a king. Suddenly he bolts, but Boaz follows him, and while the rest of the deer run in all directions – a distraction gambit, perhaps, to protect their king – and the pack of riders behind me follow them, Boaz has only one quarry in mind. He is flying now and I have my crossbow set and ready. Suddenly the king stag stops. Boaz, in full flight, takes longer to come to a halt. And there we are, the two of us, two kings facing each other. And all the symbolism stands there before me. Two kings locked in battle. And only one can win. In the distance I hear the whoops of hunters, the twang of bowstrings and the thwack of bolts hitting their mark or piercing the trees. But all of it is at a distance, or so it seems. Here it is simply the two of us, and the whole world has slowed. Two mighty creatures, but only one in God's image; only one anointed by Him. This gives me power over this other king, over all other kings. The bolt flies. I have released it without knowing.   It is an instinct.   He watches me with those large brown eyes hooded by long female lashes, and then he staggers and falls. The noise he makes brings the world back to time. I hear them approach.

- *The king has him. The king has him.*

But I say nothing.

HAROLD GODWINSON - THE LAST SAXON

DREAMS

The house in Islip, where I was born just after the new century began, is shrouded in mist. It so often is in the early mornings, standing as it does where the rivers meet. But today the mist is thicker. Bodies are hidden by its wraiths and only sounds penetrate. My father is away from home, as so often he is, fighting against the Viking hordes who want to prise from him the throne of England. My mother has left us in the charge of our nurse; Alfred, Goda and I must make up our own amusements. The mist doesn't frighten us. We are used to it. We use its wrappings to enhance our games, playing hide and seek. As the oldest of our mother's three children, I feel a responsibility for them, but I enjoy the squeaks and squeals they utter when I jump out at them. But this morning, the game has turned sour. The mist is so dense that I feel certain my brother and sister are no longer in the woods, playing our game. They will have returned home, and I am alone here. I am not afraid, but the damp makes me shudder; it penetrates my woollen tunic and I feel cold and clammy.

Suddenly, from out of the mist, a huge brown figure appears. His head is covered by the hood of his deep brown cloak. Only his eyes shine in the darkness. I am afraid. I stand still, hoping to make myself invisible to him, but I know he has seen me. His voice, when he speaks, is deep and resonant.

- *Edward. Prince of England.*

The man kneels before me. His dark eyes are level with my own. There is something familiar about him. Something that eludes me, like the mist itself.

- *What is it you want with me? And why do you come out of the mist to frighten me?*

HAROLD GODWINSON - THE LAST SAXON

- *I come to give you praise, Edward.*

The sound echoes around me, as though man and voice are not one and the same.

- *Then you should do it on a clear day when there is nothing to fear.* I try to keep my voice calm, though I am still quivering inside. *My father would punish a man for accosting his son in such a manner.*

- *Your father has nothing to fear from me. You have nothing to fear. I have come to proclaim you King of England.*

To be King of England would mean my father is dead and I would have heard if something had happened to him.

- *Have no fear, Edward, your father still lives. But you will succeed him. You will return this country to its Saxon heritage. You will become a mighty king. You will become a holy king, a saintly man.*

And then the mist swallows him up. My head spins. What has happened here, in the middle of the woods, less than a bolt's flight from my own home? Who was the old man? Is he a prophet? If he is a prophet, then I am to be king. Or is he simply a figure of a child's imagining?

As the mist clears, I see that I have wandered close to the old mill and the church of Saint Nicholas lies just beyond it. Thomas, the old miller stands outside of the mill, with his son, Robert, a boy of my younger brother's age, but who is already taller and stronger than me. They each have a hand on a sack of corn, left by the villagers to be ground. They look up as I approach.

- *Did you see him? Did he pass by here?*

They look at each other and then back towards me, emerging from the woods.

- *We saw no-one, Prince Edward. No-one has passed here since we started to unload these sacks.*

HAROLD GODWINSON - THE LAST SAXON

I look beyond them, towards the square wooden church. They return to their sacks and I pass them along the cart track back towards the village. The church door is open when I arrive, but inside it is dark and empty. Once my eyes accustom to the dark interior, there is enough light streaming through the windows, set high in the walls, to see my way down the aisle. And there he stands, the figure in brown. The statue of Saint Nicholas, with his hooded head, and his piercing eyes.

Since my boyhood days Saint Nicholas has appeared frequently to me, guiding me with his wisdom. It was the saint himself who told me to build the great church at Westminster. He had come to me the day of my succession, reminding me of the promise made to me as a child. And it was to Nicholas I prayed to today. I was not in Islip, but at the altar of Saint Peter. The Witan had summoned me to a meeting. It was to be held in the palace and as always, I preferred to pray for God's wisdom before listening to these self-appointed wise men. God would give better advice. Nicholas, known by all as the wonderworker, had led me here, and he would lead me onward. I keep the Witan waiting as long as I can. I am the King, anointed by God, as foretold by his holy saint. When I arrive, the meeting seems already to be under way. Godwinson is present, as I knew he would be. As I enter, they look up and I can see the guilt in their eyes. They are plotting.

- *Forgive me, gentlemen. We were with God and Saint Nicholas. What have we missed?*

HAROLD GODWINSON - THE LAST SAXON

The Witan looked at the Earl of Wessex, then he spoke.

- *We need a new decree. More taxes need to be raised.*

- *More taxes? Surely our people have paid enough taxes to the Vikings. Do they have to keep paying now that they are gone?*

It was Everwin who spoke. I remember having asked him what his name signified: *Wild boar friend* he had told me. I joked that I too had to befriend many wild bores, but Everwin is not renowned for his sense of humour – nor are the rest of the Witan.

- *There are incursions from across our borders, Edward. The Scots and the Welsh have armies posted at our gates.*

- *And is England not protected by my good earls – by Northumbria and by Hereford.*

Harold bristles behind Everwin. I know he hates to be reminded of his duty. He takes a step forward, and I raise my hand.

- *I will speak with Everwin, and the Witan. Harold Godwinson, you may take your leave. I know you will have spoken your views to these wise men.*

The anger burns red hot in his face, but in the presence of these elected counsellors, he knows he must yield. It is agreed. The people of England will pay more, and I will meet with Harold and his brother Tostig, Wessex and Northumbria. In the quiet cool rooms of the palace, the two earls lay out their plans. Once, long ago now it seems, I would have envied them their planning, their war preparations, but now it is tedious and I can only see dead Saxon bodies. Is this what a king must do? It seems so, if he is to protect his people – and his God – from pagans across the borders. After Harold has departed, to muster his forces against the Welsh, Tostig remains.

- *I have a separate matter to bring to you. One of a more personal nature*

HAROLD GODWINSON - THE LAST SAXON

- *We are here to listen to our subjects, Tostig, earls or peasants alike. What troubles you?*
- *Hakon lies in a Norman keep, a prisoner of the bastard duke.*
- *My cousin is his host. I know nothing of prisons.*
- *Hakon is my brother's son. Hakon is your step-nephew, much-missed by the queen. Is it not time to bring him home?*
- *He was given as hostage against your father's plotting against me. It was Queen Emma, my mother, who took him to Normandy with her. Even after her death, the Norman duke reveres her. Will this nephew not return with his deluded claims of being descended from Cnut, as his father did? Do we not have enough threats in the kingdom already? In return for Hakon, I pardoned your father and returned to his sons the power and titles you now hold. He has his uncle, Wulnoth with him. No harm shall come to him.*
- *But England has need of him. He is my nephew and he is a loyal subject of the King of England.*
- *Surely there are enough of Godwin's tribe here in England already. But in the name of your sister, in Queen Edith's name, I shall seek his return to us.*
- *Will your majesty allow me...*
- *There are noisy Scots to kill, Tostig. When they are quiet, I will send word to Normandy.*

I feel his impatience and it is wearing. I dismiss him with a wave, and stop his bleating.

That evening, Edith comes to me.

- *I have heard of your conversation with Tostig.*
- *Is nothing secret in the kingdom?*

- A queen must know her husband's thoughts, as any wife must. Thank you, Edward. I miss my brother Sweyn, and Hakon will bring me some solace.

- I swore oaths of allegiance to Cnut. I did not extend them to the sons of his Norman wife.

The King of Alba stands tall and grim, his sword hanging at his side. He looks for all the world like a bear; shaggy beard and rough fur-coat open at the sides, the bear's head balanced where his crown should be. Every inch of him resembles the fabled berserkers – the wild Viking warriors who haunted our woods in the army of Cnut. I am mesmerised by the bear's mouth, teeth stained with blood.

- And will you swear such an oath now, Macbeth Ri Deircc?

- My only oath is to my Alban people. Your armies must disband; they must return south.

- And if they will not?

The huge figure lifts his sword and I feel its keenness as it slices through my neck.

When I wake, my clothes are dripping with sweat. The King of Scotland haunts my dreams. I have never seen him, but his image is burnt into my memory just as surely as if I had faced him in battle. It was his head that had been removed from its shoulders, while mine remains safely attached. Though, at times, it does not feel any more secure.

The dream is no less vivid, even now that I know he is dead, has been dead for some years. Tostig, leading his newly-acquired

HAROLD GODWINSON - THE LAST SAXON

Northumbrian troops has done as ordered. They have returned to clear the borders, but only with the help of Danish forces. Their presence in Northumbria is a threat, far greater than the Scots. But Tostig reassures me that they are allies. They pose no threat to us.

In Wales, Harold was dealing with threats to our borders. His resolution was no less bloody and a new spirit came to haunt my dreams. Ealdgyth, the Mercian widow of Llewellyn, shows me her hands. The bright emerald reflects the light, blinds me. Blood drips from her fingers as she removes her ring and replaces it with the duller blue stone. Her wrists are bound in chains, and the man who holds them is only too familiar. On her head she wears a crown, my Edith's crown, the crown of England.

Harold has returned and is knelt before me, alongside him a new bride. The rewards of war. Her fingers are bare, her head unadorned.

- *The Welsh are defeated, King Edward.*

- *But not all of them are dead.*

I see he takes my meaning, as his head turns towards the woman.

- *Ealdgyth is a daughter of Mercia. Her marriage to Wales…*

- *We know of the arrangement, Harold. We were party to it. She was offered to Wales to bind our countries. She is as beautiful now as she was then. A king who has forsworn the marriage bed still has eyes for a beautiful woman.*

- *And now she is home...*

- *And has agreed to be my wife.*

- *But you are already married. To Edith.*

- Edith and I were handfasted, Edward. It was never a marriage in the sight of God.

How quickly a man will turn. She is a beautiful woman, this Ealdgyth, and Harold is right. His marriage to Edith was never sealed by God.

- And this marriage will be in the sight of God?

Harold looks at his conquest. I signal her to rise and I can see she is as elegant as she is beautiful.

- I will accept no husband other than in the house of God, King Edward. I have been a Queen and now I shall be the wife of Wessex. Willingly.

Even as she spoke, I feel the earth shake beneath me. This move of Harold's presaged something – more than just a marriage. This is jockeying for position.

- Let a little time pass, Ealdgyth. Time to mourn a dead husband and king. Time to move from widow's weeds to bridal gown. Time to show us your loyalty.

That night a new dream came. A beautiful queen with hands of blood, rings of green and blue, who wears the crown of England on her head. I have ruled England for more than twenty years, but my hold on the crown feels suddenly less secure.

William

HAROLD GODWINSON - THE LAST SAXON

CAPTURE

The castle walls at Caen are thick. Beyond them, I can make out the sails of the ships in the harbour. Harold Godwinson has been brought in chains. Alongside me, the boy Hakon – in truth no longer a boy, with early signs of a fair beard - watches. Wulfnoth, Harold's youngest brother, no older than his nephew, is not with them. He has become a Norman, in his dress, in his loyalties. Hakon believes that Harold, his uncle, has come to rescue him and Wulfnoth, though neither is in danger here in this castle. I see beyond this. Wessex has no love for Hakon, despite his ties of blood. Hakon's father should have ownership of titles and land that Harold now has. Hakon is in greater danger from his closest kin than he is from me. And it is Harold himself who is in danger, daring as he has to come into this lion's den. I have not fought off all those who would have taken Normandy from me, to stand afraid of this English earl.

I try to recall this Earl of Wessex from my journey to England over a decade ago. Back then it was his father who had stood in my way. He had intervened in my talks with King Edward, and although I had received the assurances I sought - that I would succeed the childless king - it was clear that Godwin would oppose my claim. Now here is his son, a fiercer opponent by all accounts, determined to dispute my claim. But I have him now, here in my castle walls, and we shall see which way he will jump.

I hear the door opening behind me, and there is Harold Godwinson, flanked by Ponthieu's men, and Count Guy himself holds the rope that binds him.

- *We caught a fish, William. A big catch, don't you think? The storms drove him into Ponthieu, blown off-course from his journey to Caen.*

HAROLD GODWINSON - THE LAST SAXON

We salvaged him and his men from the sandbanks; drowning rats pleading for their lives.

I look at the captive. Even in this precarious position, he has a proud, wilful demeanour. I cannot imagine he would ever have begged for anything. This Earl of Wessex is a dangerous beast. I frame the words carefully in my head.

- He is rightfully your prisoner, Count Guy. Why do you bring him to Caen?

- I had expected you, William, to answer my summons to Ponthieu. I would gladly have handed over this English rat there. Instead you have forced me to bring him here. I don't want his Saxon hordes coming down to Ponthieu to rescue him. He has been well tended in the hospital, and he has recovered from his injuries.

While Ponthieu speaks, I watch his prisoner. He stands still, erect. I turn my attention back to Guy.

- What recompense do you seek for turning him over to me?

- None, William. I offer him as a sign of my fealty. Ponthieu is a loyal subject. Besides, what use have I for a Saxon rat?

- Nevertheless, Guy, I shall reward Ponthieu for this act of loyal service. Release him to me here, and then we shall make you our guest. A feast will be given tonight in honour of this deed.

Guy bows his head, and hands over the cords that bind Harold into my hand. He leaves the chamber. I look at Hakon. He is trying to seek eye-contact with his uncle but Harold continues to look directly at me. Once again I gather my thoughts.

- Harold of Wessex. Why are you here, in Normandy? Why do you come like a thief in the night?

I am told that my accent is strong; that it is sometimes difficult for foreigners to understand. But Harold has understood.

- I came to rescue my kin. Wulfnoth, my brother and Sweyn's son, Hakon. Both were young boys when they were taken hostage by the Queen. We believe they are being held captive to secure your claim to England.

Hakon watches his uncle; I think I see a ghost of a smile upon his face. Turning back to Harold my mind is busy, phrasing, preparing my words.

- And you come with armed ships to snatch him away?

- I came prepared for a dispute, Duke William, but I came with Bishop Leofric who is hardly a warrior companion.

I know Leofric. He succeeded the Norman Bishop.

- Leofric is your Archbishop of Canterbury. I know him to be a pious man.

- Unfortunately, his piety did not prevent us being shipwrecked. He has suffered some mishandling at the hands of Bishop Odo, and is being tended.

- Edward has promised the kingdom to me. Why should I require a hostage to secure what is already promised?

- Edward is childless, but this may not always be the case. He will have a natural heir.

- We know enough of your England to know that Edward is sworn to a life of celibacy.

- What is sworn can be unsworn.

It is plain enough. Harold Godwinson has plans to be regent, at the very least. Any son of his sister, Queen Edith, will be watched over and schooled by the Wessex clan, and Harold is their leader.

- Our bishops assure us the marriage was never consummated.

- Leofric will tell you otherwise. He was there at the bedside. Their marriage was made real in every way. There is even talk that Edith is with child. She and the king have been reconciled.

A lie. Edith is in a convent and Edward spends more time astride his horse than his queen. But I will say nothing of the network of spies we have in England.

- Then we shall, all of us, pray for a happy conclusion.

Now I shall need to choose my words carefully.

- Should God continue to frustrate even so pious a man as King Edward, then know, Harold, I am the rightful heir. Edward has sworn it to me. We are kin; my grandfather was the king's uncle, both of us linked to the late Queen Emma, the king's mother. Who in England has a better claim? It is so. Even our city is named by the Saxon King Arthur, who is held in such reverence.

- Then you need detain us no longer. Hakon will return with us. If Wulfnoth, as it seems, prefers life here in Normandy, then I shall not rescue him against his will.

- There is a ransom already sent to England for your release, Godwinson. You will remain here, as my guest, with Hakon, until the ransom is paid.

- And Wulfnoth?

- He wishes to remain here. Speak with him.

- Wulfnoth is named for his grandfather. Our mother misses him and begs me to return him to her.

- Ask him. He is of an age when he will come or go as he pleases, unless you will take him hostage?

I watch him. He is not afraid. He knows that the money is already sent for.

- My brother, Tostig, is already on his way, Duke. The ransom will be paid as you have requested. Until then…

I hold my hand up to silence him. He speaks too freely in another man's castle. Besides, I know that Tostig has left for England rather than risk his own capture. There is no ransom.

- Perhaps you do not know that Tostig has returned home. He shows little filial loyalty, Godwinson.

I can tell that such news had already reached him. He had not supposed I knew it too.

- There is more you can do for me, while you are here, Harold. I have had chambers prepared for you adjacent to your nephew. You will be untied and free to enjoy Norman hospitality. Tomorrow we shall talk again.

- Norman hospitality is not as charitable as you may think, William. This is a cold castle with cold gaolers. But I shall take you at your word.

I take my knife from its sheath and cut the cords.

- See. You are free to wander these cold walls.

- Until tomorrow then, William. Come Hakon. Embrace your uncle who has come to bring you home. Let us go together.

When they have departed, the room seems to expand, taking up the space the Earl of Wessex has left. Harold has a reputation as a warrior. He can be of use to me here in Normandy before he returns.

The horses are ready. The army waits on us. We shall ride against the Duke of Brittany. That Duke must be taught a lesson – once and for all.   He has invaded border lands near Mont Saint-Michel, and not for the first time he threatens Normandy. Harold and his soldiers are on one flank. He will see how enemies of Normandy are treated; he will be part of my army. I know his reputation, and his skills will be valuable in the battle that is to come. I summon him for a final time before we set off. He sits high in the saddle; he is a valuable ally but I must show him that he will be foolish to oppose my claim to England. What better way than for him to see up close how this Duke of Normandy deals with his enemies.

- Tell me again, William. Who is this Conan?

I take time to reply, choosing my words with care and caution.

- He is a man of poor judgement, Wessex. He ignores my warnings, and still he crosses our borders and threatens to steal lands from me.

- You have a long-standing rivalry with Brittany; is that not true?

- I see that Wessex is well versed in the politics of Northern France. We have treaties in place; Conan breaks those treaties and wants to steal what is rightfully mine.

- You are, Duke William, a man who has a clear sense of what is his…

- I am, Harold. And I have the force to ensure that promises are kept.

I can tell from his face that he understands me. He turns his horse back towards his men, then takes a look back at me.

- And when this skirmish is fought, when Conan's nose is bloodied and his force retreats back to Brittany, then you will release me, my men, and my nephew?

- I am a man of my word, Wessex. I have said so.

- Then let us proceed, for I am impatient to return to England.

The army moves forward, horses leading the way, with the foot-soldiers behind us. Before nightfall we see the great spire of Saint-Michel, towering high above us. It had been won in battle more than a hundred years ago, by Longsword, my ancestor, and I will do his memory justice today. We arrive at the river Cousenon, with its fearsome reputation for mudbanks and quicksand. There, on the other bank sits the Breton army, their tents pitched, their flags raised, but their army still not set. An attack now would rout them, and send them home. I hold up my hand. The army stands still. They can see the host on the far side of the river and they are impatient to fall upon them. Harold, leaving his place in the line, rides towards me.

- *They seem unprepared for us, William. They must know that we are here, and that we mean to fight them.*

I know why they are not lined up against us. But Conan is in for a surprise.

- *They think we cannot cross until the sun has baked the mud hard. They think they are safe for another two hours.*

- *Will we wait then, until they are ready to fight us?*

- *No, Harold. We shall hit them hard. Now, when they least expect us.*

I lower my arm, and the foot-soldiers raise their halberds and roar as they run across the sandy bank to destroy Conan's army. Harold sends his men after them. Over two hundred men, with the lust for blood in their throats, screaming and shouting with enough noise to wake the devil himself. I watch as the Breton men crawl out of their tents and stand, unbelieving as the invasion force nears the mud flats that stand between us. The river is dry here, and the men barely get their feet wet. Suddenly they stop. The mud is clinging to their ankles, then clawing at their thighs, as they begin to sink. Harold appears suddenly, his mouth shouting commands.

- *Sound the retreat, William. You will lose your army in the quicksand.*

Retreat? With Conan at my mercy? But he is right. We will never reach the other bank. Some have already started to drag themselves back, bodies covered in slime and mud. Harold himself returns to the edge of the mudflats. He dismounts and I watch him slip wicker shoes over his boots, then run, like a man crossing snow, towards the place where the mud was deepest. I kick the horse's flanks and the mare takes me forward. Ahead of me, Harold has pulled three men from the grip of the quicksand, and my horse senses the danger too and rears. It catches me unawares and I slip from the saddle. I land, heavy, winded, bruised on the mud, and I feel it sucking me down. Soon there will be nothing left of me except my helmet. I call out and Harold turns his head towards me. He finishes pulling a soldier free, and the man follows the others, crawling on his belly to cross the sucking flats. Harold, his shoes spreading his weight more evenly, turns back, and runs, as best he can, towards me. His arms are under my chest, heaving at me. He is fighting the weight of my armour and the force of the sand. I am sinking, sinking, sinking.

The battle is over. Conan has retreated with those of his men who have survived. The mud baked hard for us to cross, and then the river returned. On our way home, Harold and I take our rest within the walls of Saint-Michel, while the soldiers occupy the tents left behind by the fleeing Bretons. Conan has escaped my anger but he has learned his lesson. We have chased him as far inland as Dinan, where he cowers behind the city walls. Norman land is forbidden to him.
I have had time to think how I shall reward the Saxon Earl, for there is no doubt I would have died beneath the mud, but for his bravery. I had already sent for a cache of weapons, gifts for my saviour, and

perhaps there is more I can do. I have seen this man in battle. He is a good man to have on my side, but he will make a fearsome foe. I need to ensure that we will never be on opposite sides in battle. Alliances need to be made. I had set out to make this Saxon Earl aware of the might of Normandy. Instead, Harold has seen my weakness. But he is still here in Normandy, still in my castle, and with Hakon he remains until I release him. Before he leaves I need to extract a promise.

OATHS

- Am I still your prisoner, Duke William?
I let the thoughts come before I reply.
- You are my guest. And like Hakon, your nephew, we shall make you welcome until you leave Normandy. Besides, I have knighted you, renewing a tradition started by your King Arthur. Your bravery at Saint-Michel has not gone unheralded.
- Then I am free to leave.
- Not quite yet, Harold.
Before he can speak again I turn my back on him and speak to the assembled guests, and to the guards that flank the walls of the castle hall.
- Make this Saxon Earl welcome in the court.
I turn slowly back to him, all the time rehearsing the words.
- And when you are refreshed, Godwinson, return to me so that we may talk about your safe return to England.
When Harold returned it was dark, and the tables were laid out for the feast.
- This is in your honour, Harold. We treat our English cousins well.
- The richness of your table Duke William only serves to remind me that it is time to return home.
- I would prefer it if you stayed at court awhile. You will be treated well, in line with your position as Earl of Wessex, and family of the King of England. There is much for us to discuss.
- The weather is conspiring with you, Duke William, and persuades me to stay.
Throughout the feast I watched as Harold's eyes constantly drifted to my daughter's face. Matilda and I had already noted his interest in our daughter, Adeliza. It was the Duchess who had suggested the betrothal. If I can persuade him, get him to propose marriage... This would be a surer guarantee of Edward's promise. Harold would be

my son-in-law, and while Edward remained childless, it was his best chance of sitting alongside the throne.

The feast continued and I left Harold and Hakon to themselves. Watching them together, it was clear that Hakon and Harold, while related by blood, would never be close friends. Harold knows what I seek. He knows that if he wants to return home – alive that is – then he must give me what I request. Norman food is rich and savoury, so a few months spent in this realm might win him over. In the meantime, Matilda and Adeliza will visit him regularly. Adeliza is still young, not quite thirteen, but she knows her duty and she knows how to present herself. She is at the right age for a betrothal. Her mother is already planning the nuptials.

It is some time later that I summon Harold, this time without Hakon. It is dark outside and the torches as well as the fires have been lit.

- *Tell me Harold. You have spent much time with my wife. What is it that you and the duchess talk about?*

Matilda sits coyly behind me, her hands in her lap. There is a smile on her face. We have rehearsed this moment.

- *We have been plotting behind your back, my lord.*

Harold watches to see the effects of his words. But I give no sign of concern.

- *So it would seem, Wessex. And what plots do the two of you hatch?*

- *The Duchess, your noble wife has been matchmaking.*

I turn my shoulder towards Matilda; it is all I can do to keep the smile from my face. Does this Saxon think a Norman Duke and Duchess can be divided so easily?

- *I am already wed, Duke William. And Edith and I have sons and daughters, some the same age as Adeliza.*

- *I have heard that your wedding is not legitimate in the eyes of the church. You were married in the Danish way.*

- *Legitimacy is not everything, Duke William, as you yourself can testify.*

HAROLD GODWINSON - THE LAST SAXON

Harold Godwinson betrays his disdain for me with such a comment. I know what he is thinking. How can an illegitimate duke raise such an issue! I will say nothing. I try not to let my thoughts paint themselves on my face.

- *My daughter is very young to be wed, Harold.*
- *I have agreed to our betrothal. And I shall return in five years for her hand... if you are in agreement with your wife.*
- *We have talked about this, Harold. There are no secrets between us. It will be a good match: for Normandy, for England, for Wessex, and for Adeliza herself.*

Harold smiles. I read his mind... It is an easy matter to make a betrothal here, under duress, and to break a promise back on safer shores. But this betrothal will not be so easy to break.

- *She is a girl with much beauty, your daughter... and she is truly devout.*
- *She is her mother's image, Wessex, and she will grow even more fair.*
- *Then I shall be blessed by such a union.*

Silence falls about us again. Our words suggest the two of us are in agreement, but our bodies speak with greater honesty. I speak slowly and deliberately so there can be no mistaking.

- *And as my son-in-law you would have no reason to oppose my claim to the throne of England.*

How will he react now that all my cards are placed on the table before him? This was the real matter, the crux.

- *On what, Duke William, is such a claim based?*
- *It was promised me. King Edward himself sent his Holy Archbishop to give the news, to make me his heir.*
- *And you fear the promise may be forgotten, William?*
- *I fear that, though he is a good man, Edward may not be able to resist the temptation to give his throne to a Saxon Earl.*

Harold knew his place. He knew his safety depended on his reply. What he said was:

- If what you say is true, then be in no doubt, as your son-in-law, I should not oppose such succession. Indeed, I would welcome you, William, with open arms. You have my solemn word.

I have extracted his promise, here before witnesses. What he thinks is certainly somewhat different. Back in England, where his base is strong, such an oath, made under duress, would count for nothing.

Adeliza was furious. She most resembled her mother, when she spat fire!

- I will not marry him. He is an old man. He has a wife in England, and some of his children are older than me! He is half Viking. I will not marry him. You cannot make me. I would rather marry Hakon. I thought it was your plan...

I take a step towards her and raise my hand. I watch her flinch as I slap her cheek.

- You are my daughter. You will obey my orders or you will spend your life in the company of other women. This marriage will secure our family's place in England. With Harold Godwinson at your side, my succession is made more certain.

- But Harold is not a good man father. He has been, at night, with other women, women from this household.

- Harold is a weak man, but a strong earl, Adeliza. It his earl's strength I seek.

- But Hakon is his nephew. Surely if he and I...

I have heard enough. This headstrong daughter will do as she is told. It is bad enough that there are enemies beyond my gate. I will not have opposition within my own walls.

- Hakon is nothing. He has nothing, except some spurious claim to be Old Cnut's grandson. How would such a union benefit us?

- How would my marriage to an old man benefit me?

My hand rises again, but she turns on her heel before it reddens her face again. I turn back to Matilda.

- Speak with her. Make her understand.

- She is her father's daughter, William. Once her mind is made up…

- You must unmake her mind. She will be betrothed to Godwinson. She will marry him on her eighteenth birthday. She will secure my rights to the English crown.

- I will speak with her.

- Do, Madam. Make sure she understands. Our daughter will obey my will.

A letter arrives early one morning. It is Spring now, and the weather is more conducive to a return trip to England, and I have agreed that Harold and Hakon can return together. The messenger has been captured and his letter intercepted, and now it is in my hand. It is a mother's letter to her son: Gytha Thorkelsdóttir to Harold Godwinson:

My dear boy, Bishop Leofric, your companion in Normandy has sent me a letter. It tells me what has transpired there, and I await your reports. Wulfnoth has become Norman and your brother Tostig has left you there. And now Leofric hints that you are in danger of succumbing to the Duke's wiles. What of Adeliza? Will you forsake your Saxon family? Your wife? Your children? If what he says is true you will be lost to us all in England. Tostig is planning a rebellion against the king, and I am left with your other brothers and the girls to secure your father's legacy. You must return home. I need you here. You must find a way to break with this bastard duke, this Norman, and return home. And soon. The other earls are busy in your absence. They speak long into the night with the Witan. They will try to force Edward to name his successor at their next meeting in London. Edgar is preferred, Ironside's grandson. Next week your year and a day are up. If William will not release you, you must escape.

I give him the letter. Harold looks at it, turns it in his hand.

- The seal is broken.

- The messenger was intercepted. Secret letters are brought here – when they are found.

I allow him time to read it. I watch him as he reads it, much more quickly than I. The Saxon language is alien to me, but there are many in the castle for whom it is the native language, and they have told me the detail of its contents.

- My mother seeks my return.

- Then you must return.

Harold holds his mother's letter between thumb and forefinger:

- It says that the Witan are persuaded to support Edgar's claim.

- I know its contents.

- Then it is in your interest to let me return. Only I can prevent it.

- And you will represent my interests.

- They will be my interests too, with this betrothal to Adeliza.

- Come with me today to Rouen. Swear before my bishops that you will uphold my claim.

- There is too little time, William, for such games.

- It is the cost of your free passage, Harold.

HAROLD GODWINSON - THE LAST SAXON

He finishes the letter, folds it and places it with care into his tunic pocket.

- *Come then, let us do it. I must return home. Tostig is loose again, and The Witan need to be told what they must do.*

I have been at great pains to assure my claim. I have taken Harold to swear his allegiance on the holy relics at Rouen. I speak the oath first:

- *I see you, Harold Godwinson, and I call you here this day to return to you this ransom and name you a free man again.*

He takes my place at the altar. His words have been rehearsed:

- *I see you, Duke William. I thank you for the time spent here in your lands. I have been treated well as you promised.*

He stopped. There was silence and we wait for him to continue. High above his head, motes of dust float in the sunshine which streams through the windows. I look at him, urging him to complete his oath.

- *I know you wish me to swear allegiance to you as heir to England, but, as I am sworn to King Edward I must refuse.*

Suddenly there is uproar. I turn my head to the guards who flank the walls...

- *But...* Silence falls again... *I will swear to you, William of Normandy, that if my king dies without heir I shall swear that Edward named you as his nominated heir. I can do no more. I will do no more.*

I turn aside. Just behind me, to right and left, stand my advisers, experienced in oaths and other legal matters. I wait for them to confer by looks and smiles, and then in unison they nod.

HAROLD GODWINSON - THE LAST SAXON

- It may suffice, Harold Godwinson. I shall draw up a document recording your promise, and both of us shall sign it. This must be a holy oath, Harold, that you must keep at peril to your soul.

I stretch my hand out to him, and he takes it. It is done. He has sworn on the finger bone of Saint Nicholas. Not that he was aware of the relic at the time, but later, when it was revealed to him, when he saw he had been tricked into it, he only smiled. Both of us saw the irony of an oath taken in the name of his own king's patron saint.

I had honoured him with a coat of ceremonial chain mail and a coronet in the fashion of Alfred's crown. The bishops hid the relic beneath the altar cloth. I am not sure that Harold will keep such an oath of fealty, but before witnesses, clerics and nobles, he has given his word. To break such an oath would call his honour into question. So the door is doubly locked. On one hand a religious oath, on the other a betrothal. Both are binding, and Harold will be held to account for them.

It has not made for a peaceful household. Adeliza keeps to her room. She refuses to speak to me. She has begged me to change my mind, to release her and Harold from the betrothal. I am adamant, as a duke must be. Especially a duke who is destined to be King of England.

HAROLD GODWINSON - THE LAST SAXON

PRAYERS

- We must pray for peace, and prepare for war.
- Armed with a book and a sword, no doubt, William, as was Saint Paul.
- He was a man not unlike myself. A man in need of a change of image.

Harold is gone from Normandy. He has sailed back, his fleet much humbler than the one that brought him here. His younger brother stays here, by his own choice while Hakon has gone with him. He carries with him my hopes for a peaceful succession. And I pray for peace.

Matilda and I are on our way to Bayeux to meet with Bishop Odo. Matilda has planned the creation of a huge tapestry and hopes to convince Odo of its merits. Although he is my kin, my half-brother on my mother's side, he will still need some persuading. Matilda's plan is an ambitious one and will cost much. I have long wondered why we in Normandy have not taken the habit of our Viking cousins of appointing court poets. These skilled versifiers serve their purpose well, making sure that the stories that live after their masters, show them in a more golden light than might otherwise be the case.

Growing up with the title of *William the Bastard* has not necessarily provided me with the best start in life; but perhaps it has been the making of me. I have had to fight hard – literally as well as metaphorically – to establish my right to rule. And where this was in doubt, force of arms has secured my place. Some men, and I count among them, Edward of England, can inspire love and loyalty. Others, like Harold Godwinson, and William of Normandy must rely on power and might. This journey to Bayeux is an attempt to change the common view of me. It is all Matilda's idea, but it requires Odo's support. Odo can be a difficult man to please. Odo has power; as an ordained man, he has support from the church. As a soldier, he is a respected and brave warrior. And although he owes his position to me, I must treat him with respect and dignity.

The journey is half a day's ride from Caen and, as we approach, the walls of Odo's project stand tall. It is clearly unfinished, but it has an imposing feel and will add much to Bayeux and to Odo's status. The Bishop is there to greet us. His large hall is richly ornate, showing him to be a man of Mammon as much as a man of God. He himself is a tall man, well built, a little more than my own height, but less broad. He is a strong and powerful man. He looks as though he himself would have the strength to lift the buckets of stone which each day are hoisted to the top of the walls of his new cathedral. He is an ally, respecting our kinship; he would be a fearsome enemy. Odo knows my ambitions; he himself has ambitions. I remember, one late evening in Caen, when we shared a few cups of wine together, sharing our hopes and dreams, one of the few times I have allowed my tongue to be loose in his presence.

- *You think Edward will keep his promise, William?*
- *I think he may be ill-advised to renege on promises made.*
- *You will attack England if you need to?*
- *We must pray for peace, and prepare for war.*
- *Armed with a book and a sword, no doubt, William, as was Saint Paul.*
- *He was a man not unlike myself. A man in need of a change of image. And what of you Odo? What are your dreams?*
- *Dreams are for those people who lack power, William. I do not dream, I plan.*

- And what plans do you make?

- Plans that will help secure your position. He stopped for just a moment before adding: *And plans that will put me at your side. William and Odo. Together we can conquer this island of yours if need be.*

I remember his words now, as we stand together, arms held in warm embrace. Matilda steps between us.

- My Lord Bishop, if I may intervene.

- Of course, my Lady. Come inside and look at the plans that have been drawn up for this new cathedral.

- I want to talk with you about creating history.

- Then nowhere could be finer to do so. This cathedral will rival many for its glory.

- This is a different type of history.

Matilda takes his arm and leads him through the huge space that will eventually be the great door. I am aware, of course, of her idea. A tapestry. Not just a giant cloth to adorn the walls of our castle but one that tells a history. Its length will cover the walls of this new cathedral. The story that unfolds will show how William and Matilda rise to become King and Queen of England. Of course, the story is not yet fully told. There is no way of knowing how it will emerge, but already she has ideas of how it will begin. Then in a series of scenes, over fifty Matilda proposes, the story of King William will be told. It will show everybody, and for generations to come, how bold and brave a man is this Bastard Duke of Normandy.

- And who will pay for this elaborate embroidery, Duchess?

Like all good churchmen, Odo was always interested in the price of things.

- You and I together, Bishop will commission its creation, and my ladies at court will embroider it, here at Bayeux, and it will adorn the walls of your new cathedral. Most of these women came from my home in Flanders, where we have a long tradition of creating such objects.

Odo's eyes looked along the length of the walls, at present barely above his ankles, and saw how it would look adorning the walls of his great cathedral.

- Matilda is a real asset to you William. Where you look to the next day, she spies eternity.

Odo is right. Matilda has always been thus; able to look ahead and judge present actions in terms of their future consequences.

- So, Bishop, what do you say to my offer of immortality?

- I say, Madam, that history remembers only the winners. If William becomes King of England, then the tapestry will be remembered. If he fails, then...

- My husband will not fail, Odo. England is promised to him and now the only man who stands in the way of such a promise returns to England having sworn an oath of allegiance. This will end well, I think. Edward is a Norman at heart. His youth was spent here and he trusts William more than he trusts the Saxon earls who jostle for power.

Matilda puts more faith in Harold than I do, she is always more trusting. Odo is more like me. He sees the need for contingent plans.

- I will share the costs with you, Madam, so long as my part is recorded within its stitches.

- Your height and girth are not so great, Bishop Odo, that we cannot spare enough thread.

And she gives him her hand, and turning to me I see that smile. She has won him over, as I knew she would.

- *And now, Bishop, I shall take advantage of your famed hospitality, which by reputation surpasses even that of our Duke at Caen.*
- *You flatter me, Duchess. But I shall do my best.*

I watch Matilda as she leaves, stepping over masonry, carving a path through dust, to the door of the Bishop's palace. Her belly shows the early signs of our seventh child, but she makes no allowances for it. A perfect mother, Matilda seeks alliances across Europe; the perfect wife, she supports my ambitions. When she has left us, Odo comes to stand beside me. I am still looking at the plans.

- *What do you think, William? Will this not prove to be a wonderful cathedral?*
- *I am more interested in castles than cathedrals, Odo, but it looks to be fine and will buy you a place in heaven.*

Though I am turned away from him, I know he is smiling. He takes my arm and I turn back to him.

- *I suspect we may need to be ready for war, William, just in case.*
- *You are a wise soldier as well as a good bishop...*
- *And with that in mind, William, I suggest we start immediately on the commissioning of another project.*
- *Another project, Odo?*
- *A fleet of ships that will put fear into the heart of the Saxon people.*

Matilda, having finished her breakfast, is waiting for me. She has news of her project. The early scenes are drawn in preparation.

HAROLD GODWINSON - THE LAST SAXON

- What do these early scenes show, Matilda?

- They depict Edward instructing Harold to cross the Channel to meet with you, William, to give to you the rights of succession. There are scenes of the storm, Harold's capture, and how he swore his oath of allegiance over the holy relics of St Nicholas.

- You have done well, Matilda. And have you managed to draw Odo into the story?

- He meets with Bishop Leofric at the time of his capture by Guy of Ponthieu. He is well-drawn.

- And what of Harold's bravery at Mont-Saint-Michel?

- It is depicted too, William. Harold rescuing sand-sunk soldiers.

- And what of me? How am I shown?

- As a brave and noble warrior. You are the centrepiece of the story. I have drawn your likeness, a handsome, rugged man.

- I am probably flattered by such depiction, Matilda.

She smiles and takes my hand. She is excited by her project, and I am satisfied that this tapestry will give me what I crave too, a place in history where all men will see how William the Bastard became King of England.

Harold Godwinson has arrived in England and has gone to see his king. Information flows across the channel like flotsam, so I know he is meeting with King Edward. There are troubles in England – when are there not? – and Tostig has shown his true colours, supporting the claim of Hardrada of Norway. That raises different issues, and the fleet which is being built quickly now, may be needed to fight Vikings rather than Saxons. My sources tell me there are already Viking men in the north of England who will take up arms against their king to bring a Viking ruler back to London. These traitorous Saxons fight amongst themselves, and now Tostig, King Edward's brother-in-law seeks to bring back Viking rule to England. Whatever the outcome of any such battle, the victors will be weakened and ready to be crushed by our invasion force.

There are signs of great activity on the river Dives. Bishop Odo is working with William of Poitiers. He has convinced them of the need to support me in the assurance of land and titles in England. I am still praying for peace but the ships are being built. From all I have heard, Harold presents as a conundrum. A man of excellent standing in England, or at least that part of England he controls, and a man who hunts with the king. And yet he seeks the crown for himself. I know it to be so. He has never forgiven Edward for the banishment of his family which he believes led to his father's untimely death. Loyal and cunning: two sides of the same coin. Even this man has his own scribe. His deeds are chronicled where mine are not. I share these thoughts with Matilda, who reminds me that the tapestry designs will change all that. Her eyes are bright when she tells me her latest news.

- *I have reports too, William. Harold seeks a new bride. He means to marry the Welsh Queen, a conquest of war. He is fearful that the Saxon people will not accept Edith Swan-neck as they were handfasted, in the Danish way. Some of the earls use it against him saying he is more Viking than Saxon.*

- *And what of his betrothal to our daughter? What of Adeliza?*

- *He will break that oath, William. It was made under duress. It will please Adeliza, and may improve her temper.*

- *Tell her nothing, Matilda. She stays betrothed. We shall wait until I am King of England – then we shall see what his oath is worth.*

A man who can break one oath can surely break another. I say nothing of these doubts to Matilda. Let her continue with her project. The Tapestry can show my place in history. There are men loyal to me who know Harold's mind. If praying for peace does not work, then I must prepare for war.

HAROLD GODWINSON - THE LAST SAXON

PREPARATIONS

- We must pray for peace and prepare for war.
I have called a council. William of Poitiers is invited and other nobles. They come together not out of love but out of duty, and fear. They are gathered here, today, at Caen, to decide whether we should prepare for an invasion of England. But there will be no debate. I want no debate. We are to prepare for an attack on England. I hope such an attack will not be necessary – indeed I still pray it will not be necessary – but we are to prepare. They know, all of these greedy noblemen, that there are rich pickings to be earned and their greed will outweigh their fears. I will warn them that Harold Godwinson means to deny us all. I shall have what is promised me, and I shall hold Wessex to his oath. But I have seen this earl and I suspect his honesty; we shall prepare a fleet bigger than any he has seen and if the sight of its arrival does not force him into obeisance, then our Norman soldiers will persuade him. That is why they are here, these warring dukes. I need their support and I will use their greed to buy it. Matilda stands with me, close, in the Great Chamber; she already assumes the bearing of a great queen. Though certain we cannot be heard over the noise of eating and greeting, we bring our heads closer, until we are almost whispering.
- Have you received the assurances you sought?
- From the Holy Father?
- From Alexander…
I hold aloft the parchment scroll which had arrived by messenger only yesterday. I had feared its lateness. I wanted to have it here for this gathering.

HAROLD GODWINSON - THE LAST SAXON

- It has his seal. They cannot oppose it. The Pope remembers his Norman cousins. We put him in power and now he remembers us.

- The assembly will approve, seal or not. Look at their greedy faces.

- But with it, Matilda, we have the highest authority. God himself is on our side. We shall march under the Pope's banner. Who then will oppose this invasion?

- The English will, husband. Harold Godwinson and his Saxon hordes will oppose us.

I turn my attention to our guests. They have finished eating and their talk is more serious now. I must act before their courage fails. I call them to attention – a single blow of my hand on the table yields silence. I have them now, in the palm of this same hand. I allow the silence to hang, preparing my words with care and caution.

- So my lords Poitiers and Jumièges, how have you decided? Are you in support of such a venture?

- An invasion will cost many Norman lives, Duke William.

- Our invasion will cost more Saxon lives…

Fists bang on the table in support. I know how to gain these men, win their support.

- … and reward our Norman dukes. England is ripe for picking and we shall pick it clean.

- And the Pope supports us?

I hold the bull aloft.

- I have his seal. Signed by The Bishop himself, 'Servant of The Servants of God'.

- And the Holy Roman Emperor?

- The young Henry blesses us, and promises his support.

Poitier smiles. He knows I have sought such a blessing. He raises his hand again to speak.

- And what of Sweyn, the Norway King? Would he not rather support Harold against us, and then deal separately later with his Saxon cousins?

Now for my final argument – the most convincing of all. The dukes who sit assembled fear defeat more than anything. They do not want to support a lost cause and if I am beaten in England, they do not want to be at my side. They would rather be here in Normandy, fighting over my lands and title, like ravens attacking a bloodied carcass. I take my time then like some magician pulling a jewel from his ear, I give them what they want.

- Sweyn is with us. Sweyn's blood is our blood. Are we not Normans – men from the North just as he is? And though we are different branches, our roots are the same. Vikings and Normans will not oppose each other. They will stand together. Besides, I know this Harold Godwinson. He hates us, but his hatred of Norway and Denmark runs deeper. He remembers the Viking raids, the crippling taxation. He will not seek support from that quarter.

Their fists hammer again until the noise fills the Great Chamber.

Later, when the dukes have dispersed, when allegiances have been sworn, and when fleets have been promised, Matilda and I stand alone. She looks at the letter from the pope.

- Where is the signature, William?

- It will come, Matilda. It will come.

- But you told them…

- And they believed me. Pope Alexander will sign, but probably not until after we are successful. He only backs the winners.

- And Sweyn?

HAROLD GODWINSON - THE LAST SAXON

- Will never support us. Norway has its own interests. I hear news that Harald Sigurdsson plans his own attack on England. When Edward dies, Sigurdsson will strike.

- And what of you, William?

- If the Witan do not welcome me to London I will wait for the noise and the distraction to launch our own invasion. You saw them here in the chamber. With all of us together there will be no stopping us. Not Saxons, not Vikings. And we shall fight under the papal banner, and with the support of The Holy Roman Emperor. Who will stand in our way?

- Then perhaps the Confessor will instruct The Witan to do its duty, and there will be no need for war. Perhaps Harold will keep this oath, though he has broken his marriage promise.

- And as King, I shall do penance for my deceit.

I take Matilda's hands in mine, and turn her to face me. She has such strength, and now she will need to show it.

- I must give my time to the preparations, dear wife. In my stead you must hold the reigns of Normandy. These loyal dukes will seize on any lapse on our part, any looking away, to steal our power from us. You shall be Normandy, while I prepare to be England. I know you are strong enough for such a task. Place Robert at your side – his is almost fifteen and handles a sword like an experienced soldier. It will be his destiny one day to be Duke of Normandy. Let his duties start here.

HAROLD GODWINSON - THE LAST SAXON

So there it is: pray for peace and prepare for war: the book and the sword; the tools of Saint Peter. I have moved out of Caen and I spend my time at Dives. Odo and I visit the harbour there regularly. Money pours in from the dukes, and the ships grow in number daily. The bishop and I spend much time together, and our conversation is often of Harold of Wessex. It seems that King Edward is ill, lies waiting in London for his death and martyrdom, and Harold stays close by. He has the ears of the Witan, and we suspect it is not my name that he practises on his lips; it is not my cause he promotes. Rather, it is his own. Jumièges maintains there are three hundred ships and they will be ready to sail from Saint-Valery as soon as they are required. I doubt there are so many, but he claims that number and I have paid him accordingly! Now we must wait. It is winter now and the storms that churn the sea between England and Normandy are the Saxons' best defence. Odo talks with me long into the nights. He has news every day of events in London, though I know nothing of his sources. Edward has no love, it seems, for his queen. Her family connections - her father, her brothers – give him cause to doubt her loyalty. She is Queen Edith, but she is also Edith Godwinson, Edith of Wessex. Then there is Harold himself. He is heir to all his father's fortunes, and he has taken the reins of power. He was once the second man in England. Now he has climbed higher still. The king's power is held in his hand. There are Godwins everywhere. They hold four of the six great earldoms. They think they are untouchable, for isn't their sister the crowned and anointed queen? But Harold and Tostig are at loggerheads. It was Tostig that had been sent with the ransom for his brother. But it never arrived. And now Tostig throws in his lot with Hardrada. He has his eyes on a quarter of the kingdom, his prize for treason. Harold will never forgive him. First his brother Sweyn, then

HAROLD GODWINSON - THE LAST SAXON

Wulfnoth who is loyal to us here, and now Tostig. This man who would rule the Kingdom, cannot even rule his own house. But Harold still wields great power. Godwin had been called king-maker, this son of his is known as law-maker. The king busies himself with hunting, while the Earl of Wessex rules the land. And he is ripe for chopping down.   It is time for the other earls, jealous of his power to throw him off his pedestal.   And then there is the question of his so-called marriage to Edith Swan-neck. Odo shows his anger.

- *Harold Godwinson's hand-fasting ceremony will be his downfall. It is not just we Normans who question its legitimacy. Despite their six children, he is forced to look elsewhere.*

- *I have had news of this. He swore a betrothal oath to our daughter, but it seems he is not a man to be trusted.*

- *You know how it is, William. In their youth, men marry for love and lust; in their middle age they look for sounder reasons.*

- *It seems his visit to Normandy changed him. I take no pride in it. Who am I, known still, by those who dare utter it, as William the Bastard, to talk to him of legitimacy? He has shown his disdain of me; perhaps his conscience is pricked. If he has sights on kingship, he will need to vouchsafe the legitimacy of his heirs.*

Odo smiles and raises his hands in mock piety.

- *Harold would be well-advised to remember his oaths, William.*

- *He has been so advised, Odo. We must see to it he listens and pays heed.*

And this time it is not Odo the bishop who smiles, but Odo the warrior.

HAROLD GODWINSON - THE LAST SAXON

Matilda and the children are at Caen, and Christmas preparations will be in full swing. Advent is half through, and the castle will already be buzzing with excitement. Our children love the holiday. Holly rings hang on doors, and fires roar. The farms, lying under a blanket of early snow, have released their hands for idler pleasures. Riding through the woods and fields that stretch away from the coast, I can see how the season draws to its climax. It is good to be returning home. It is good to think of things other than England and War. It is good to think of family. What will next Christmas bring? Will I still be William of Normandy, a bastard duke? Or will I be William of England, a legitimate king? Even this far from the coast, I can feel the winds blowing across water. Winds of destiny. Perhaps I shall be proven wrong. Edward, on his deathbed, will name me as his heir; Harold will ride out to welcome me, arms outstretched, and the fleet assembled and readied at Dives will not be needed. I fancy I can hear hollow laughter, Saxon taunts. *Come if you dare, Bastard Duke of Normandy. Come if you dare!*

My hand grips more tightly on my sword; my reins are released a little and the horse responds to the spurs that kick into its flanks. Hooves fly, making tracks in the snow, like the wake of my ships. I am ready – like Advent I am preparing. If the call comes, I am ready. But if the gauntlet is thrown down then I shall pick it up. It is my destiny to be King of England. I shout to the winds, throwing my words back towards England.

- I am ready.

Ealdgyth

HAROLD GODWINSON - THE LAST SAXON

WEDDING

Small steps. Small steps. One foot in front of the other. I am no stranger to such a walk. The aisle is strewn with petals, and on either side sit all the greats of the kingdom. Except that the king is ill. But the queen is here, in his place at the head of the church. Harold's sister.

Small steps lead at last to the altar at the great Winchester Cathedral. I would have preferred Westminster, but this is the seat of Wessex power. Christmas is close. There is snow outside, and inside are signs of preparation for the season. Holly and mistletoe hang over the doors and festoon the statues. It is all green and white, as am I. Green dress and white coronet. I look at Harold beside me. He stands tall and fills the space with his presence. Together we make a fine couple. Courtly, perhaps even royal! It may be a marriage of convenience but it is not inconvenient!

I do not know how one is supposed to feel about an upcoming wedding when it is the third one. And each was an act of political expediency. Hywel ab Edwin was my first husband. I was little more than a girl then, and my mother and father saw it as a perfect match for their daughter. More importantly, of course, it was a perfect match for them. Father was ambitious. He wanted to retain his hold as Earl of Mercia, and the power and wealth it accrued. But he wanted to keep the Welsh on his borders quiet. My marriage to the king of the southern areas came with status as well as security.

Unfortunately, father backed the wrong side and when my husband was killed by the ambitious Gruffudd, I returned to Mercia and lived the life of a widow.

HAROLD GODWINSON - THE LAST SAXON

Growing up, I saw little of my father, and my mother had died when I was still a child. My grandmother, the Lady Godiva, was my guide. She was a bold and brave woman, who dared to defy her husband, Leofric. The stories about her riding naked through Coventry were probably true. I never saw it; I was in Wales with my first husband. I remember once asking her. We had gone together, Grandmother, Father and I, to Saint Mary's in Coventry.

- *That story they tell of you… Is it true?*

I could feel rather than see her smile.

- *What does the story say, Ealdgyth?*
- *That you rode bareback through the streets of the city.*
- *Bareback?*
- *That's what I heard, grandmother. At the Trinity Great Fair.*
- *Certainly the horse was bare-backed.*

It seemed such an inappropriate thing to do – laugh whilst kneeling at my grandfather's tomb – but it was funny.

- *But not you, grandmother?* I asked, once I'd gained some composure. *You were not naked?*
- *It would seem a very brazen act for a woman married to an earl and a strong belief in God.*
- *It does seem so, grandmother. Very brazen.*
- *So look at me, Ealdgyth. Do I seem the brazen sort to you?*
- *You are fearless, grandmother. Everybody knows that.*

The stories told how she had ridden out in defiance of Leofric to protest about the taxes levied on horses. She would say no more about it. The rumours would live on of course.

- *And what of 'peeping Tom'? Wasn't he a tailor who disobeyed the edict to stay indoors?*
- *It's a remarkable story, don't you think?*

- Not for Tom. He had his eyes put out.

- A remarkable story.

Story or not, *Godiva's Ride* as it was called, always came up when people knew she and I were related.

I was a widow for thirteen years. The second wedding, ironically, was to my first husband's murderer. Gruffudd ap Llewelyn, to give his full title, had taken the title King of Wales, and my father had helped him secure the crown, joining him in Ireland to recruit a large army. That was the second time I saw Gruffudd. He was a tall man, with a shock of red hair. With my father's troops alongside him, he defeated his last rival, and became King of Wales, the first with such a title. My father had returned to England and King Edward, in return for the peace he brought to the western lands, and, for the anger it provoked in Harold Godwinson, restored Mercia to him. We were back in Coventry, and back in power.

- A marriage to the Welsh king would be a fine match, daughter. Your sons will be kings.

- I have already married one Welsh king, father. These kings do not hold on to their crowns, or their lives, for very long. He may be dead before we have an heir!

- Then marry him quickly and give him an heir.

- And you will be grandfather of kings.

- I have known what it is, Ealdgyth, to have power. And I know too what it is to have it stripped from you; to be banished by a king. I seek greater security for my children. You are your grandmother's child. I see in you all the strength she had. You are a perfect match for a king.

And I was, though it may be immodest and un-ladylike to say so. I was a good queen. Supporting her husband and bearing him children. His son Owain brought him the greatest happiness. It was the death of my father that led to the battle that killed my second husband. I returned to Mercia under my brother Edwin's protection.

Like all of us in Mercia, I had grown to be wary in the company of Harold Godwinson and his brothers. When Tostig was thrown out of Northumbria after alienating all the people there, it was my younger brother Morcar who took power. Any rise in Mercian influence was seen as a fall in Wessex power. So when I first met Harold, I needed all the strength and courage of my grandmother. I remember the meeting. Edwin had been summoned to Westminster. King Edward had called all his earls together and I was asked to accompany him.

- *We are to discuss the security of our borders. Who knows the Welsh better than you, sister? You may have something to offer the king in that regard. Besides, we shall be sorely outnumbered by the Godwinsons, and we need to show the power we have.*

- *And I am part of Mercian power?*

- *Of course, sister. And you know the Welsh mind.*

- *I knew my husband's mind, Edwin. This new king...*

- *You will accompany me, and speak if you are asked to do so.*

Harold Godwinson, the Earl of Wessex, was a tall man; fair-haired and blue-eyed, he cut an impressive figure in the hall. He stood – literally – head and shoulders above the rest. He sat at the king's side, and was seen whispering asides to the Confessor, like a sinner in church. I know he noticed me. I have been told many times that I am a woman of beauty, and I cannot deny I have used my beauty as a weapon. I caught his eyes upon my face and held them with my own eyes. It was he who turned away first, and it was he who smiled at me first. His wife was not present in the hall. I knew her by name and reputation; she was Edith the Fair, and she was pious and loyal. And she had borne him sons. But there were rumours too, that their marriage was not blessed in church and by some at least was seen as unlawful, illegitimate. And that applied to his children too. Perhaps when they had coupled, it had mattered less, but now, in this new England, where a 'living saint' ruled, perhaps he was fearful of losing the family dominance in England.

It was clear enough at this gathering where the seat of power lay. The king looked older than his years; his skin was pale and he seemed to lack interest in the proceedings. I saw Harold point at me, and the king beckoned me, called me forward.

- *You are Edith of Mercia, are you not?*

I kept my head bowed and nodded. Now was not a time for boldness; now was a time to play a womanly role.

- *You were once wed to the Welsh king, were you not?*

- *I am the widow of Gruffudd ap Llewelyn, King Edward.*

- *Why do they continue to threaten us?*

- *They believe your majesty is a treat to them. They seek peace but will wage war to find it. It was the Earl of Wessex who struck the first blow.*

Harold's face turned crimson as he rose to his full height. He was angry, and certainly not used to being challenged by a woman.

- *It was beneath King Edward's own banner that I fought the traitor Gruffudd. He swore oaths to live in peace and not cross the border. But he broke those oaths.*

Edward held up his hand and Harold returned to his seat.

- *Is that true, Ealdgyth? Did your husband break the promises he made to us?*

- *He crossed into Hereford many times, King Edward. Mostly to accompany me on visits to my family.*

Edward's raised hand kept Harold in his seat.

- *And did he come with force across our borders?*

- *The King of Wales feared the build-up of soldiers in Hereford and along the border. He feared what it would mean for him and his people. He feared an attack. And Kings who are afraid will sometimes act rashly and unwisely.*

- *I had a father like that. As his name suggested, he was poorly advised. He was in continual fear of attack. It led him to make bad decisions.*

- *Then you will understand.*

- *I know what is reported to me. Your husband – the late king – broke his promise. I sent Harold of Wessex to deal with him.*

- *And Harold of Wessex left me a widow, King Edward. And now this same Harold is poised to fight my brothers.*

- *Tostig was given rule over Northumbria by me. These rebels, some of whom sit at the council today, are opposing my will.*

The king, with a wave of his hand, sent me back to my seat. He turned to talk with Harold, their heads close together again. Then we were dismissed.

It was later, when Edwin returned, that I discovered the outcomes of the meeting. My two brothers were joining forces to evict Tostig from Northumbria but Harold would not join his brother. With England squabbling, it would be a good time for the Welsh and the Scots to cross the borders. Harold would be sent to Hereford to keep watch on the Welsh. He would leave his brother to fight Mercian forces without the Wessex forces.

The battle was short but bloody. Tostig was captured and the King was forced to accept his banishment. The rumour was that he had gone to join Hardrada in Norway who was preparing an army to invade England. Harold supported his king's actions. This was the second brother who had tried to oppose the king, and each time Harold had shown his loyalty was to England rather than to his family. Harold had gone to Hereford and struck a deal with the new King of Wales. When he returned, he visited me in Coventry.

- It is good to meet you again, Harold of Wessex.

He came with gifts, and news of his plans had preceded him.

- It is good to meet you again, Queen Ealdgyth. This time on better terms, I hope.

- You killed my husband.

- I did my duty, madam.

- And I mourn his death.

- But a woman of such beauty will not be a widow for long, I think.

- My father is dead, Harold. Any match will be mine to make.

- And do you seek a match?

- My bed is cold at night and it would be pleasant I think to have someone warm it.

I saw him smile. It was a very warming sight. But I was not done with him.

- *By contrast, your bed, I think, is very warm. Lady Edith is known to be both fair and fecund.*
- *Edith and I are happy together, but you know that we are not wed in God's eyes.*
- *The Danish way… Yes. And she is of Danish blood I think.*
- *Which mars her in the eyes of many. By contrast you are the grand-daughter of Leofric, a Saxon earl.*

It was a strange proposal, but at least it was made to me.

- *And if I accept your proposal – for I assume that this is a proposal of marriage?*
- *The king would like to see Mercia and Wessex come together.*
- *Ah. I see. Another marriage of convenience.*
- *Only if it is convenient to you, madam. I would not want it any other way.*

All my life, Wessex and Mercia had been at loggerheads. The king himself had set one earl against another, and now it had come to this.

- *I would become wife to Wessex as well as sister to Mercia? In this way you will secure the support of Mercia and strengthen your own links to Wales. You see, Harold, I know how this game is played.*
- *You would also be the queen's kin, and who knows what other titles may follow?*

I saw his ambition there. It glowed on his face, shone from his eyes. He aims to be king. And he wants me to be his queen.

HAROLD GODWINSON - THE LAST SAXON

HAKON

My brother's nephew has few of his uncle's traits. Hakon is short, no taller than me, and dark with a thick black beard. Harold tells me that he is the image of his father, and with the same temperament. I never met Sweyn of course, but by all accounts he was a headstrong and truculent man. And Hakon is certainly like him in that. He spends most of his time here at Senlac drinking and sleeping. Which doesn't enamour him to his uncle Harold. We have spent too many hours arguing about him.

- *He needs something to do, Harold, something to make him feel part of this family, to feel needed.*
- *His father was the same.* This was my husband's standard response.
- *That doesn't help. To be honest with you, Harold, I don't feel altogether safe in his company. He is something of a womaniser...*
- *His father was the same. It is this humour that brought us down in the past. Hakon himself is the product of a lusting father.*
- *Give him something to do. Surely there must be some part he can play in Wessex affairs.*
I hadn't intended any pun, and Harold was not in good humour.
- *I don't know if I can trust him. He favours Tostig over me, and I fear he will betray us.*
- *Then why do you allow him to stay?*
- *It is my mother's wish. She says that the boy is all she has left of her eldest son...*
- *Hakon is no longer a boy.*
- *To my mother, we are all boys. I can't just abandon him.*
- *Then use him, Harold?*
- *What use can this boy* – he sees me open my mouth – *man be to us?*

- He has knowledge of Normandy. Find out what William plans.

- He tells me nothing.

- Then perhaps I can help.

I have watched Hakon as he watches me. I know he desires me, and my status does not cool his lusts. Perhaps I can use his desires against him. Get him to talk.

- If you can get him to talk to you about William, that would be of service to all of us, including the king. But be wary of him. He is just like his father.

And even as Harold stomps away, I can see Hakon watching me from the dark corner where he sits. Always he lurks in dark corners. He watches his uncle's retreating back and then sidles his way towards me. It is all I can do to stop my flesh from crawling...

- He doesn't like me.

- Your uncle is concerned about you. He took a great risk rescuing you from William's clutches.

- There was no need to rescue me. I was in no danger there.

- You are safer here, surrounded by your family, by Saxon men loyal to your king.

- My father should have been king. William told me how my father was robbed of his birthright.

It always comes back to this. Hakon believes that his father's claim to be the illegitimate son of Cnut gives him, Hakon, the right to be the next king especially as Edward has no heirs.

- When I am king...

- Hakon, you will never be King of England.

- When I am King Hakon, Harold will know what it is to be disloyal to my family.

- How has Harold...?

- He had my father banished; he caused my father's death. Now he has banished Uncle Tostig, the only other man in my family who believed in my father.

- You are here because Harold recognises your kinship.

- I am here because he doesn't want me to stay in Normandy where I can be of use to William.

- Then be of use here, at Senlac, in England. Be of use to your king in London.

- Harold would never permit me to meet with King Edward.

- Tell them what William plans. You know his mind, and Harold believes he is a threat to England.

- William believes Harold is a threat to England.

- William is a Norman. What rights has he to the English throne?

- Edward has sworn to make him his successor. There will be no natural-born heir, and through the late Queen Emma, he is closer to the King than any other. Besides, Edward has sworn to it. And when he becomes King of England, William will remember those who have helped him.

- You refer to yourself, Hakon?

His answer was a smile – more a lascivious grin. When he did speak, it was all spite and malice.

- When William hands me the crown, those who opposed my father, those who have mocked me had better stand ready to meet their fate. Perhaps, lady, you would make a better queen… and he licked his lips, which drooled.

I need to leave the chamber. Hakon is a monster, waiting for his chance to strike. But I stand my ground.

- Know this, Hakon Sweynson. You will never be King of England, and if I am to be queen it will not be at your side. But you do have a future here, if you will but see sense.

- What future is there for me – an orphaned bastard, son of a disgraced earl?

- You will inherit lands and titles. It is what Harold wants...

- It is what my grandmother wants.

- It is true. Gytha wants you to be the earl your father failed to be. Tie yourself to your uncle's fortunes, and it could still be so.

- Everyone says that Uncle Harold will not rest until he wears the crown...

- And if he does, who better to take the title Earl of Wessex than the son of his eldest brother?

From his face, it was obvious he had not considered this possibility. Perhaps I had caught him now. Perhaps he would be more willing to serve Harold's cause.

- Go to him. Offer him your service. He is waiting for you.

I watch him as he moves towards the door. He takes a last look back, and the smirk still sits on his face. But Hakon knows where his advantage lies. Not with a duke some fifty miles across the sea, but with his uncle, the Earl of Wessex, here in his father's homeland.

- I don't know what you said to him, but Hakon has come to me and sworn his service. I have told him I will place him head of a troop of men from our eastern lands. If he proves himself...

HAROLD GODWINSON - THE LAST SAXON

Harold and I are in our bedchamber. He takes off the woollen tunic and lays it on the bed. It is a cool day and I can see the goose-bumps on his flesh. Steamy breaths accompany his words.

- *And how are the preparations for the Epiphany Feast?*

We have scarcely recovered from the Christmas celebrations. We are not a family given to much revelry, but the earl has a duty to his people to hold a feast and reward the loyal. And now Epiphany is close. Throughout the day local landowners have been assembling and this evening their earl will thank them for their service. The hard-set snow prevents any work on the farms so they can be spared their duties there. These minor lords still see Edith as their mistress. Here is my chance to show how things have changed.

- *Everything will be ready. Except you. Take time to relax before our guests arrive later in the week. They will want to see you at your best.*

- *I shall be at my best, Ealdgyth. Be sure of that.*

- *How does the King?*

- *He suffers bouts of delirium. He has sent for my sister, then when she comes, he sends her away. I fear this king will soon be ready to be shriven.*

- *Perhaps he will listen to his own confessions?*

- *This is no light matter. I am to be summoned by The Witan if his condition worsens. I think word will come soon.*

- *And will he name you successor?*

- *The Witan will do as the King commands.*

- *Then all the more reason to welcome our guests tonight. This may be our last such gathering here at Senlac.*

- *Give me a little while. Meantime, go and play the hostess.*

He kisses me, full on the lips and embraces me. Standing there, held between his strong arms and powerful chest, I feel safe. Surely no harm can come to us, whether he be king or not.

- And is Edith ready too, with your children?

- She is ready, Ealdgyth. And she knows her place in the proceedings.

Edith has been remarkably calm despite her change of circumstances. There are plans in place for her to return to Walsingham, though the children would stay here with us at Senlac. She is resigned to it. We speak together every day, and she is a rare woman. I find no resentment in her. She knows that her marriage to Harold may hinder the future he has mapped out for himself. His fate will secure the future of her children, including the unborn child still in her womb, so she takes the pragmatic course. I don't know if I could be so forgiving.

I see the riders approaching. From the banner they carry, I know they are from the king. Perhaps this is the summons. I go downstairs to greet them, send servants to tend their horses.

- We are sent by the Witan, Lady Ealdgyth. We are sent to bring Harold back to London.

- He is expecting you. Come let me order you something to eat.

- There is no time.

Harold enters. He has replaced his woollen tunic.

- Come, sirs. Let us return to the king.

Hakon lurks in the shadows. It is from the dark corner that he speaks. He always seems to inhabit dark corners where his face cannot be read.

- Take me with you, Harold.

Harold takes a moment to consider then replies.

HAROLD GODWINSON - THE LAST SAXON

- Be ready for a fast ride. We must be in London before tomorrow night.

And Harold and Hakon, together, follow the messengers into the night. I hear the hooves retreating, and they are gone. It seems I am to play host tonight – perhaps Edith will be hostess.

King Edward is dead. Hakon has returned and brings a letter from Harold, and a command that I am to go, and to take all the children to celebrate a coronation. We are summoned to Westminster Abbey. We are to travel at once. My fingers tremble as I break the seal and unfold the letter.

King Edward lay dying. With all the Earls of the Kingdom, I stood by the bedside. It was just as I'd feared. The old man had not put the seal in any hand, the ring on any finger. How many other claimants would appear when the Confessor took his last breath? This would be a death for England as well as its king, and a bloody one at that. I swear to God I would not have done as I did if a successor had been named. I watched the rise and fall of the King's chest, slow, weak. There was no doubt he was dying and I knew I must act fast if I was to take what was to be ours. I had to be sure that darkness and chaos would not follow. The Witan will support me but I need to make it clear that I am the king's chosen successor. A plan formed in my mind. Many see me as the strongest, safest option of all the claimants. Yes, the Witan would support me, but they might need my intervention. I stand vigil over the king, and I call the king's valet to stand with me. I promised to send him if the king wakes.

HAROLD GODWINSON - THE LAST SAXON

The bedroom emptied slowly. Old men shuffled out into the crisp cold night. I signalled to the valet to close the door fast behind the retreating backs, and called him to me.

- Stand and watch with me, boy. Give your king due reverence. Keep awake, and watch with me.

And together we stood, heads bowed, as the old king slept. I knew he would never awaken from this sleep. I waited until the early morning hour; the young man's head slowly drooped. I took up a place next to Edward's bed and leaned my ear to the king's mouth. The breath was stale and weak. He reeked of the afterlife already. He said nothing. He had already begun his journey to sainthood.

I called the groom.

- You are witness to his words!

The boy looked confused, still emerging from his sleepy state.

- My lord?

- You heard him speak… just then… into my ear.

- My lord?

- You were awake, were you not?

- Yes my Lord. I was awake. I am awake.

- Then you must have heard his last words.

- His last words, my lord?

- Commending to my protection his widow and his title, his country. You must have heard that if you were awake.

- Yes my lord. I heard the king speak.

- Our friend and king is dead. You must go to the Witan; they are still assembled in the Great Hall. Tell them what you saw, what you heard. I saw the confusion in the boy's face. And he saw the sword in my hand.

- I will, Earl Harold. I will go straight away and tell the Witan it was as you have said.

- No, boy. You will tell them it was as you heard! Or will you tell them you fell asleep on this night?

- I will tell them what I heard, my lord. I will tell them.

And the boy scrambled away, down the long, shadowy corridors to report that the King and the Kingdom had passed. So we are to be crowned. At Westminster.

I fold the letter and look at Hakon.

- Do you know the letter's contents, Hakon?

- The seal is unbroken. Lady Ealdgyth.

- Do you know its contents?

- I know that King Edward is dead. And soon the world shall know.

I watch his face for the hint of a lie. But this time, at least, I believe Hakon speaks the truth.

- The old king is dead and Harold, your uncle, is proclaimed king. There is to be a coronation, on Epiphany, at Westminster Abbey. The old king will be buried and the new king crowned.

- With unseemly haste, it seems.

- The Witan are afraid that any delay will bring a new war of succession.

I can see his mind working fast. He is trying to assess what this means for him.

- What will you do now, Hakon? Will you come with me and swear allegiance to our new king?

- No, mistress. I will go instead and find Tostig. He is sworn to oppose Harold. He has thrown his weight behind Hardrada, the King of Norway. He has promised me a share in the kingdom.

Hakon leaves and I know our paths will not cross again.

HAROLD GODWINSON - THE LAST SAXON

LONDON

Westminster Abbey had been completed in time. It was designed to hold the body of a dead king, a mausoleum, and so it was there that King Edward was buried. And Harold – the same day – was anointed King of England: King Harold, the second of that name. And I sat alongside him, swearing my allegiance and my oaths to God and to England. Queen Ealdgyth.

The unseemly haste is easily explained. The earls are gathered here in London to celebrate the Epiphany. To have them depart and then regather will be inconvenient; it will also give them time to raise opposition if they are so minded. Harold is right. There can be no delay. Already there is talk of opposition from foreign lands, to the north and to the south. The old king had made his wishes clear. The ring had passed from Edward to Harold, and the Witan are content that Harold had been named as successor. He, for his part, had promised the dying king that he, Harold of Wessex,would take care of the country and the queen. "Fair" Edith has returned to Winchester, with her daughters. Her sons have moved into the royal palace.

They will not be the only children to grow up here. I touch my hand to my belly in moments of idleness and feel the life growing inside me. Here grows the real heir of the English throne. In the Wessex tongue, my name sounds as Edith, and often leads to confusion. Even Harold has taken to call me by that name.

- *It is easier on my tongue, Edith.*

They have named me Edith of Mercia, both to distinguish us and to remind everybody that the great houses of Mercia and Wessex are joined. Combined in alliance, it gave Harold the force of arms he might need if Hardrada or William come to claim the crown – and take Harold's head with it. I am Queen of England but there are forces at home and abroad that would have me, and my husband, removed.

I have seen little of the king since the coronation. He has taken as truth the rumours of the Viking invasion that is being prepared and is busy organising an army, and discussing tactics. When he does return here to Westminster, it is to share with me his thoughts and plans for the battles that lie ahead.

- *Tostig knows our defences. He knows our weaknesses. Hakon has joined him and together they have gone to meet with Harald of Norway.*

- *Two Godwinsons, and both traitors. Do you have the will to kill them both in battle?*

- *Edith. I must take up arms against them. Whatever grief it brings to me, I do it for England, for stability. Tostig would have us all speaking in the Norse tongue. He thinks Hardrada will carve the country up and give him his own kingdom.*

- *And will he?*

- *Why would he? Hardrada is a treacherous man. He will string Tostig along until he no longer needs him. Even now, if my brother comes to me in peace, I would grant him all of Wessex.*

Both of us knew it was already too late. Tostig was gone and already planning his return under Norway's banner.

- *And if Hardrada comes? Can England defeat him?*

- *We can, and we will, Edith.*

Harold places his hands alongside my belly. The baby inside me is not yet showing. But...

- *Our child will follow me to Westminster, Edith. You shall be queen then mother of a king.*

HAROLD GODWINSON - THE LAST SAXON

Harold knows. Perhaps he has spies among my own ladies who know my situation? Or perhaps he is truly a divine king? I smile.

- Then you must go and prepare for what is to come. For Hardrada and for Tostig.

Westminster was a home and a prison. Now that Harold knows I am carrying his heir, I was to be wrapped up and kept safe. It is not something that sits well with me. As Queen of Wales, I had borne three children to Llewellyn. He had never sheltered me, kept me safely stored. Perhaps because he had other, older heirs. Harold was different and I suppose I should be grateful for it. But I spend the days in endless wandering through empty halls. I want for nothing. I am the Queen of England, and I am paid due respect – though there are some who would prefer to see Swan-neck on the throne. Not least Gytha, my mother-in-law. Being a Danish woman herself, she saw no reason for Harold to set aside his first wife, just because they were married in the Danish fashion. And, of course, Edith was more pliable than *the Welsh Witch*, as she still calls me. To her I was always Ealdgyth. She took pride in rolling the word on her tongue as though it were distasteful to her.

There is one name that is rarely mentioned in Westminster: William. When the duke is mentioned it is usually prefaced with the epithet *bastard*. In this way Harold dismisses his claim even to the title of Duke of Normandy. But Harold knows that the Norman forces may pose an even bigger threat than Harald's Vikings. To make things worse – and strangely congruent - Wulfnoth, another of Harold's brothers, is with William; another traitorous Godwinson. England's enemies make good use of the family's tensions and fractures. Harold believes that The Bastard and Hardrada are working together, attacking England in unison. Then they will divide the kingdom. I doubt that. Both men seek supreme power. I believe William is waiting for Hardrada to attack before making his move. If the Duke attacks too early he may have Hardrada to deal with as well as Harold. William of Normandy is playing a longer game. But Harold cannot wait to see what games are being played. When the first attack comes – whether from Norsemen or Normans – he must be ready. He was born for this. Born to be king and born to lead men.

Harold has asked me to accompany him to Wight. In the island's sheltered havens and harbours he is building a fleet.

- *We shall be ready on two fronts, Edith. When Hardrada attacks, we shall rely on our forces in Northumbria supported by your people from Mercia, who will hold York and drive the Vikings back into the sea – back to Orkney, from where I believe they will launch their attack. Here at Wight, we shall have a navy ready to repel The Bastard's ships. You see, Edith, England is ready for any attack. Your husband is ready.*

England is safe in my husband's hands. And our son, for I am convinced this growing child is a boy, will become king after his father.

Tostig remains a thorn in our side. Harold should have had him killed, but he still hopes that his younger brother will return in peace. I know for certain he will not. Tostig has ambitions. He wants to take his brother Sweyn's place as his father's heir. To Wessex and to England. He thinks he has more chance through alliance with Hardrada. And Gytha supports him. He is taking Sweyn's remains back for burial in Denmark, and Gytha loves him for it. Hakon is with him, to ensure that his father is given a place in Valhalla. No, Tostig will not return to England unless he carries sword and shield.

Harold is on his way to Exeter. There is a Council of War. Harold shares his plans with his captains, and they prepare for war on two fronts. Tostig holds no fear for me. So long as he has ambitions to be king, he needs Mercia's support, and my brother Leofric is too important to those ambitions. I have even heard it said that he intends to take me as his wife, once King Harold is dead. My skin crawls at the thought of him at my side. I would rather sleep with a real snake in my bed! Harold tells me he has a secret weapon in Exeter. Pigeons! I hate the birds; noisy, noxious creatures, leaving everything covered in their white droppings. But Harold says these are special birds.

- *My father told me stories about The Pigeon Man from Brugensis. He trained the pigeons to be homing birds. They were able to fly long distances, carrying messages attached to their little legs. Back and forth they would go. Father used the information gained in this way to his advantage. I have located his son – Petre they call him – who has similar skills as well as a love for these birds.*

I wrinkle my nose at the fact that anyone can love such creatures.

- *This Petre is now at Exeter. He has a full aviary at his disposal. These feathered messengers will help us again. There are more cages in William's camp at Dives and more too with Tostig, to keep track on him.*

- *The messages must be very short – to be carried on the legs of pigeons. I find the whole idea absurd!*

- *The writing is tiny and we use codes so that if they are intercepted… I have sent messages to our forces. They must be ready for the attack that will certainly come to York.*

HAROLD GODWINSON - THE LAST SAXON

London is full of the news of invasions. It is all premature. In the early months of 1066, England is a peaceful place, and there are early signs of spring. The new king is widely lauded. He is a Saxon King and the people of London see him as one of their own. They go about their business. I walk each day down to the river, where barges bring in such a wide range of goods from Antwerp and even from Normandy. It seems nothing stops the commerce of this city. But underneath all of the trade, there is a tension. England has known a relative peace for some years under Edward. What battles there were had been staged far from the city – on the Welsh and Scottish borders. Harold is eager to maintain the peace. But there are forces beyond his control, and they are making themselves felt in London. I have plenty of servants who could buy whatever I need at the many markets that spring up after each ship had unloaded its produce. But I enjoy moving anonymously among the traders, disguised with a hood and long cloak. I enjoy, too, knowing that Harold would disapprove! I carry my own coins too. I am proud to use them, bearing as they do, the name and head of my husband the king. It feels strange to exchange coins with my husband's head for bolts of cloth and cabbages. Among the stallholders and farmers, the talk is all of war, *hanging in the air like storm clouds*, as one woman says.

- *Mark my words. The river will be flowing with blood before the summer comes.*

I am curious to know what feeds such fears.

- *Where have you got such news? What have you seen?*

HAROLD GODWINSON - THE LAST SAXON

- The king keeps his own council. Not even the queen knows what he is up to.

- And what is King Harold up to?

- He is inviting the Vikings back to our country to murder us all.

A second woman, hearing the first, adds her own "knowledge".

- And he has sent word to the Norman bastard to come and live in London. When rumours are rife, truth usually flies out of the window. But there is some truth in this. Their fears are well-founded. But they are wrong to mistrust the king. I know Harold. I know my husband. He will lay down his life for his England. My fear is that he will have to do so before too many months have passed. Walking the streets has become more tiring. The baby in my belly grows heavier. My comfort is to have my children around me. Not Swan-neck's children, but my own: Meredith, Idwal and Nesta. They are a comfort to me. They speak in their father's tongue and the music of the language comforts me. The days are still short and the evenings are full of music and song from the Welsh valleys. It is my haven in this city. And we dance too. Nesta has learned to play the welsh harp, and Idwal plays the pipes, the sack tight beneath his arm, while Meredith sings, her voice beautiful and comforting, resounding around the walls of our home. When we are together, the city outside seems a long way away, and we are back in Wales. Our dances are more sedate now that I am with child, but when I sit to rest, Nesta rushes around flinging her arms and legs about. They are my comfort.

Early one morning Harold returns.

- Let them come. We are ready.

NORTHWARDS

The journey north begins in the early morning, passing through the Bishop's Gate. The summer sun has not yet risen, and the day is cool, the grass clinging on to the early dew. I am seated in one of the wagons that trundle behind the huge army. Alongside me, the three children, and still deep inside me, the heir to the English throne. It is an uncomfortable journey. We follow the ancient route of Ermine , paved centuries ago by the Roman armies – laid out for the same purposes; to fight the enemy. News of the Viking army follows us. Many of the villages are empty, as the villagers flee to safer refuges. The king's army is greeted with cheers, for the most part. The routine is established. Pigeons are sent out with messages, and will return to us later in the evening. Before we left, Harold had spoken at length to his mother. She had given him sound advice:

- *Root out any of your men who might be tempted to warn Tostig of your coming. You must defend York. Let Edith stay here, at Westminster. Your brother Leofwine and she will rule in your place until you return safely. Leofwine is young but if he has your ring and our name he will extract holy oaths of allegiance from them.*

I had no doubt that Gytha would be the real power behind the throne. But I had other concerns.

- *What of me, Harold? Where shall I be safe to bear our child?*

Gytha had an answer ready – she always seemed prepared. - *Ealdgyth must go with you to Mercia. She is trusted by them, for her father's name. She is the new Earl Morca's sister. She will help raise an army if Hardrada comes in force. And she will be safe there.*

It made sense. The names of Morcar, Aelfgar, and my grandfather Leofric were still revered, a powerful force in Mercia. So here I am travelling north, hot and uncomfortable, following the old Roman roads.

Our first station is in the town of Saint Alban. It has been a long march. Harold has driven them forward and we have set up camp outside the walls, on the hill overlooking the great saint's burial place. The Wessex farmers come into the camp, leading cattle and goats, and with carts laden with roots and greens. Harold had said it would happen and outriders had planned the route. We would not always manage such a long march in one day, but the army must be in York before Hardrada and Tostig.

- *The army will grow as we march, and we shall feed on the produce they bring. Not just the Wessex men but the whole of England will join us against the Viking horde. When we march we must make good progress. When we stop we must replenish our strength.*

I was happy to be down from the cart. And the children could get onto their legs again. The rain held off and the rest-days were to be relished. But within two days, with our numbers swollen and our bellies full, we set off again.

Our next stop is short, just to catch breath, take on provisions and enlist more men, in the town built around a crossroads with another Roman road and so our journey continues. Harold sends more pigeons and sends false trails.

- *Let them believe we are trailing them along the rivers. If we can get to York unseen it will go well for us. I want my army to pick the place to fight, outside of the great city of York. If we are attacked before then, before all our forces are gathered it will not go so well for us.*

So each day is fearful. Each step we take we look over our shoulders, to left and right. I have been in battle before, but never carrying such

172

a weighty burden as this. At least the morning sickness has passed; each morning bent double. Harold knows nothing of this - what man does? But I have carried children before. This new baby in my womb, almost to term, is no different, except he is destined to be the most powerful man in the world - so Harold says.

Our journey northward is surprisingly smooth, in all other ways. Long warm days, mild starlit nights lead us forward. Harold visits us when he can. When he does he stands with me under the stars and together we seek out the hunter, Orion, and his dog and the Great Bear, our fingers tracing their shapes. And Harold tells the children stories. Nesta is taken with the mythology and sits listening until she yawns herself to sleep. And then we stand together, my husband and I - not as royals but as man and wife - and he kisses me, and we speculate on whether there is a son in my womb, or a daughter.

- *It is a boy. I know it,* I tell him. *England is safe with a boy. We shall call him Harold.*

And once again, after we have rested and eaten, we are ready to move on. The stops become shorter, the marches longer. News has reached us, on the legs of our pigeon spies, that Hardrada's forces are growing as he makes his way towards the city fortress. He is gathering men, as we are, along the journey. Two parallel armies marching north. If we know they are there, perhaps, they know of our progress.

We are moving more quickly now and the men are complaining, but still the army moves and grows. At Ledecestre our wagon pulls off and we move westward. We are heading for Coventry, where a meeting with all the Mercian lords are assembling, my brother at their head. For a long time, we sit and watch as the army continues northward. We finally move off towards the setting sun. After a sleep punctuated by kicking feet, I am awake and ready to speak with the earls, ready to use my family name to persuade them to follow Harold into the battle at York. It is my grandmother's name that carries the most weight. They remember her ride through the city. She is old now and not so well, but she accompanies me.

- Sometimes, when men speak, their words are not heard. But when women speak, when their women speak, it can have more effect. We are gentler creatures, and they hear us when we use our powers of persuasion, and they mark our words. We may not drive men to war, but we make them see why sometimes war is necessary.

They have come in their droves to see Lady Godiva, and Queen Ealdgyth, together, speak in the city square. Thousands come to hear us, the wives with their men, urging them on, cheering us as we seek to persuade them to fight for their Mercian way of life. I remind them:

- They will tax us to poverty; they will take our lands and our livelihoods. We shall lose our Saxon identity and become an off-shore province of a Norwegian King.

I rouse more cheers.

- Join your king - your Saxon king - and march north to oppose the forces that would destroy our way of life.

A pigeon arrives the next morning. It is Idwal who brings it; the bird in one hand, the tiny message in the other. My son has taken on the role of pigeon-master. He has a way with animals and the birds come willingly to him, sit on his palm and wait for him to retrieve their messages.

- King Harold has halted at the Ouse. He awaits reinforcements from Mercia. What shall I tell him, mother?

- Tell him they are on their way. Mercia has listened and its men will be with him soon.

My journey is complete. The sadness I feel is that my father is not here to greet me. We had not always spoken kindly to each other. Aelfgar was a politician and a warrior, perhaps better than he was a father. I loved him, as a daughter should love her father, but I barely knew him. Even so, now that he is dead, I miss him. He had not seen his daughter rise to the lofty heights of Queen of England. As soon as grandfather Leofric was interred, I was married to my father's ally, the Welsh king, and I left home and family behind me. It was a big step and one I know he enjoyed, not just as a political manoeuvre but also because his daughter wore a crown. How much more would he have enjoyed the sight of me wearing the English crown! It would have been tempered of course by the marriage being to Harold Godwinson, the greatest political rival. He had profited from the King's favour when Godwin and his sons were exiled, and then saw his power reduced when King Edward brought them back. But now he smiles down at me; I feel it. His daughter, twice a queen, and now the most important lady in the Saxon world, even if his grandchildren are to be Wessex. I miss him dearly. By contrast, Morcar, my eldest brother, I miss not at all. He is haughty and enjoys the power he holds over the Mercians. He has no kind words for my Welsh children, and Idwal is a little afraid of him. But Morcar is a loyal subject, responsible for releasing York from the tyranny of Tostig's rule. Harold knows he can be trusted.

Coventry is my home. And though I spent too little time here after my first marriage, being here now gives me great comfort. Sitting in conversation with Grandmother Godiva is the greatest gift. The baby kicks in my womb and this gentle old woman places her hands over my belly. Her eyes are closed, her voice low.

- *Have you decided on a name?*
- *He will be named for his father. Harold.*
- *And if it is a girl?*
- *It is a boy, I am certain of it.*
- *Then he will be Harold the third when he succeeds his father.*
- *He will be a warrior prince before then, following his father into battle.*
- *And what of your other children?*
- *I had hoped that Idwal would be Prince of Wales. Tostig and Harold, fighting together, trapped his father in the high mountains of the North. It was one of the Welsh traitors who slew him, and had his head sent back to Harold, to curry favour. Now the Kingdom is divided, but I fear it will not be long before there is fighting there again.*
- *You must work towards reconciliation. My grandson will need a title to keep him secure. And the girls need good marriages.*
- *Harold will see that it is done. He is their father now and treats them as his own.*
- *And what of the Lady Swan-neck, his first wife?*

HAROLD GODWINSON - THE LAST SAXON

- She is in London but soon will return to Walsingham, and live a holy life now that we are separated. She and I are reconciled.

- You are a good queen, Aeldgyth, if you can befriend your husband's first wife and keep her from raising her children as princes.

- There are dangers everywhere, Grandmother. But I have lived with such threats for so many years. Now as queen there will be many who think that I have taken Edith's rightful place. When my Harold is born...

I feel the baby kick, almost as if he knows I speak his name. It will be just a matter of days now.

Morcar has come to pay his respects. He bows in my presence. My younger brother Edwin kneels beside him.

- I shall lead a Mercian army north. We shall take York from the greedy hands of Tostig Godwinson, and hold it in his brother's name.

- In the king's name! His brother betrays us all.

- I have sworn allegiance. Harold is a Saxon king and my sword will fight his enemies. With our brother Edwin, we shall take back the great city, and hold it against foreign armies. Harold should not be troubled. His army will not be needed. We have fought against Earls of Wessex before! The irony is not lost on me.

Morcar and Edwin leave Coventry and their army moves Northward. They will overtake Harolds's troops and take York. When their king arrives they will make a present of the city to him. It is Morcar's nature to make grand gestures. Harold will find a suitable way to reward him.

The pigeon spies are busy. There is a constant stream. Idwal reads the messages from Morcar. The battle for York has not gone well. At Fulford Gate, Tostig and Harald Hardrada have defeated the Mercian army and taken control of the city. Now Harold marches again. More pigeon-carried messages tell us that Harold is close to York. He has met with Hardrada.   There will be fighting soon.   I have lost one husband. I hope not to lose another.

King

HAROLD GODWINSON - THE LAST SAXON

HAROLD:

They have arrived, the Vikings, led by the man they call Hardrada. We shall be ready for him. It is as I suspected. Tostig has betrayed me, betrayed England, and brought the enemy to our doors. My brother and a Saxon earl. He, who should have bolted the door of Northumbria against them, has welcomed them, joined them. It begins. The battle for England.

For days now they have been building their forces in Northumbria, from the Humber to the Tees, men have suddenly found their Viking souls and followed this Raven flag. More in fear than favour, I suspect. They have tossed their coins and believe they have joined the winning side. Scarborough has fallen, so many Saxon lives lost - and I mourn each of them. Now they make their way to York. Now, it seems I must journey north to meet them. Tostig has asked to parley. I shall greet them at the city gates, but York will resist. There will be no Viking King of England.

The Viking Army is camped outside York. They expect to be given the keys tomorrow. Morcar has betrayed me.

HAROLD GODWINSON - THE LAST SAXON

YORK

Morcar has failed. The city has surrendered. Autumn has come early and with it the north winds that strip the trees, and scatter their brown husks across our path. The horses' hooves crunch them beneath their feet. The battle for York has been lost at Fulford Bridge, and now there is no choice but for me to ride into the city before the keys are handed to Hardrada and Tostig. Morcar had shared his plans with me; he and Edwin would bring their forces to bear on the Viking troops before they had time to prepare. Morcar had some doubts as to the spirit of some of the men; they had heard the stories of the berserkers, told by their grandfathers, and were afraid that the woods concealed these fearsome warriors. He had done his best to remind them that their reputation was more to be feared than the berserkers themselves. They were, after all, nothing more than wild, undisciplined warriors dressed in bearskins.

The early signs from the front line had been good. Morcar had driven the Vikings back, and on the cusp of winning the battle, the Vikings redoubled their efforts and charged against the Saxon force. Supported by newly-arriving forces, the Saxon army had been driven back. When the messenger arrived at our camp, bloodied from the battle and exhausted from the non-stop ride to relay his news.

- And your masters, the Earls of Northumberland and Mercia, are still alive?

- They are, King Harold. Both are at York. They will hand the keys to Hardrada in return for a promise that York will not be burned and looted.

- They have bargained for safe passage...

- No, my King. They have bargained for a peaceful solution.

- Ride back to your Earls. Tell them we are less than a day's ride away. I shall be in York tomorrow morning and will parley with Hardrada myself. Tell them I shall meet them at the bridge on Stamford Brook, where it meets the Derwent.

The man is given a fresh horse and I watch him ride away, until I can no longer hear the thundering hooves.

Morcar has betrayed me, has betrayed England. There can be no negotiation with these invaders. Harald will have been emboldened by this victory. If he has York he will believe that England is ready to be taken. He will make a gift of York to Tostig and then march to London to take the crown for himself. But this would be done over this king's dead body. Harold Godwinson will not surrender his country. Not while I have breath in my body and blood in my veins. My Saxon army is rested. We shall have to carry out this task alone. Northumbrian and Mercian men have fallen and few remain to join us. But Harald Hardrada will not be expecting a battle. I will turn his confidence against him. Before the sun has fully risen, we are on our way along Ermine Street.

Progress has been good. I can see the city walls and towers which stand in profile against the red setting sun. I can see smoke rising from the houses that sit just beyond its walls. Tomorrow morning we shall meet with the invaders and see their strength.

I have chosen the spot for the lie of the land. It is a good place to pitch camp. a good place to repel the Vikings if they mean to attack York. The Vikings have made camp on the far side. They know that to meet them we must cross the river. Our forces have grown and the dry Autumn fields throw up dust until it is barely possible to see the opposing army, and we will be hidden from them. I give orders for the men at the front of the line to disturb the fields and increase the size of the dust cloud. They will guess our size from the dust we create. At the far side of the brook, there are three men on horseback, ahead of their forces. I recognise the shortest man as brother Tostig. A second is not known to me but the man in the centre is recognisable from all the reports I have heard. He sits tall in his saddle, with his long yellow hair flying behind his battle-scarred ace. This is Harald Hardrada, the Norwegian King who aims to have my head on a pole. They are talking together. The size of our army has clearly caught them by surprise, and my gamble has paid off. The army is dressed in lightweight skirmishing gear. Their heavy armour and the giant shields are nowhere to be seen. As the dust settles I can see the look on their faces. Tostig is looking behind him. I know my brother. He wants to run, to retreat. Harald grabs his arm and swings him round to face us. A rider is called up and after a few moments he is sent back. He is joined by two others and I can see the urgency in their riding. They realise their mistake and now Hardrada sends for reinforcements. But it will come too late. Their Landwaster Banner is raised - the black raven seeming to fly in the breeze. A short walk brings us face to face, with just the brook between us. There is a long thin line of Viking men stretching in both directions. Their light shields are raised. Between us and them, pointed stakes have been impaled into the ground, their points ready to pierce the chests of our charging horses. Although I cannot see them, there will be archers ready to rain arrows upon us. But we are ready for them. There is still time to parley. There is still time to avoid the spilling of

Saxon blood. There is still time for Hardrada to return to Norway. Suddenly there is a commotion. Hardrada's horse bucks and the king falls heavily onto the grass. The others dismount and try to help Hardrada to his feet, but he pushes them away, clearly declining their aid. He wears a broad smile, that belies his discomfort. We are not here to make peace; we have come to present an ultimatum. Harald steps apart from the other two. Tostig watches me carefully, from behind Harald. It is the Norwegian King who speaks first.

- *You have come with the keys of York, general? Perhaps you also have the keys to London too?*

He has no idea who he addresses and I use it to my advantage.

- *I come with a message from the King of England. You will return with all your forces, back to Norway. He will forgive the crimes you committed at Scarborough.*

Hardrada laughs: a loud raucous laugh that can be heard by his troops.

- *And if I will not return?*

- *Then the only English land you will have is seven feet of ground: for you are taller than most men.* But I know this king. There will be no retreat. *I will allow you to leave - but before you go, hand Tostig over to me. He is a Saxon and the King wants to welcome him home.*

- *We are not retreating. We shall advance on Jorvik. Tostig will ride by my side and together we shall break through your army and the city walls, and the city will be burned. Unless of course you take your army and return home.*

I turn my back on him and walk back to where my horse grazes on the dew-sodden grass. I mount up and see them talking together. Tostig points at me. Now Hardrada knows it was King Harold he met. If he had known, perhaps he would have broken the rules of parley and killed me there on the spot.

The battle is coming and Harald addresses his men. They are readying themselves for our charge, underprotected. They will die here at Stamford Bridge before the sun is down.

Today is the autumn equinox, and night vies with day as to who shall last longest. So it is with us, but our day is more powerful than the Viking night. The light shall triumph. The battle starts badly for us. One of the Vikings, a brave man to be sure, single-handedly holds us back with his Dane Axe, blocking the bridge which acts as a funnel, impeding our progress. It is over an hour before he is struck by an arrow and falls back into the brook. We cross the bridge and advance on the Vikings, charging them again and again. Victory can be ours more easily if Morcar and Edwin bring the remnants of their armies to join us, but there is no sign of them.

I will not bore you, Ealdgyth, with the details, though I know you have seen how wars are won and lost. Enough to say that when the sun finally falls, it is not just its rays that make the brook and the surrounding fields red. There are fallen men everywhere, many without limbs and heads. We do our best to offer blessings to the fallen warriors but there are so many. For the most part their bodies are left where they fall. Saxon heroes of whom Saxon families can be proud.

There is further news. It is not good.

HAROLD GODWINSON - THE LAST SAXON

Some way further south, the queen pauses from reading the letter. Harold has won a victory at York. The city has not fallen but there is no word of her brothers, and she feels shame that they had not gone to their king's aid. She feels her belly. Her time is near. She is grateful to have Meredith at her side. Grandmother Godiva is helpful, but she is old. She returns to the letter.

Just as the last Viking falls - Harald Hardrada himself is carried from the battlefield and Tostig lies mortally wounded - a pigeon arrives from London. William of Normandy is on his way. His fleet is assembled. There is to be a second battle on the south coast. It seems the duke has waited and now sees the time is ripe for attack. Ships are seen on the horizon. What I had hoped would be a joyous reunion, dear Ealdgyth, will instead be a quick forced march down south again. There are boats at Wight which may hold them up, but William is on his way and he means to take our crowns and plant his and Matilda's arses on the thrones in Westminster. Even now I look to see if your brothers will join us south. Their troops, though fewer, are fresher than mine and we need them here with us. Perhaps a word from you?

Ealdgyth calls for quills, inks and parchment. She hopes that ties of blood will bring her brothers to the king's side. But she holds out little help. They are stubborn, especially Morcar, and still do not trust the Wessex men. They have long memories of times when Saxon England was riven and Wessex men fought Mercian men to the death. She is asking him to ignore history and to be loyal English earls. She is their sister and their queen - no, she scrubs through that. She is their sister and it is as their sister that she calls on them to help keep England free.

HAROLD GODWINSON - THE LAST SAXON

The rain that falls in the night after the battle, swells the brook and turns it pink, then blue again. The earth however is stained, perhaps forever. Tostig's body is found in the carnage, amongst the cadavers. My nephews, Skuli and Ketil, have been searching for their father's body, and now they bring it to me. I fold back the cloth that covers him and look at the face I know so well. I remember our childhood. I remember the day on the beach with Cnut. I remember the boy who always wanted to know… Now he is dead, as are other brothers. But this is different, Tostig died in conflict with his king - his brother but his king. The two boys ask me to forgive him. They want to take him to York for proper interment, and I am in two minds. A king must be strong and show how traitors will be punished. But a king can also be merciful. I am anointed; I am God's representative here on this little island and I must show divine traits as well as strength. I cover the body slowly taking a last look at his face.

- *Tostig. You could have chosen a different way. You were too much like our elder brother. Like Sweyn you sought to make your own path but, like Sweyn, your choices were bad, rebellious and traitorous. Now, here are your sons, seeking mercy from their uncle the king, to lay you out in ceremony.*

I cover his face again. His eyes see into my soul.

- *Take him to York, and in the king's name have him laid to rest there. But, while I can show a brother's mercy to him, I must also show a king's wisdom. Skuli and Ketil, as you are your father's sons, his punishment will be visited upon you. You must leave England. Return with the remnants of the Viking army and live among them in Norway.*

Perhaps when there is time to reflect on this time, when the kingdom is safe from Viking and Norman, I shall recall them to London. There is another boy too, who must feel a king's wrath. Ealdgyth warned me of Hakon. I expected to find his body among the Viking slain but now I am told he has joined William's armies. He has helped William prepare an invasion. I had been right all along. Hakon was a viper in our nest. So once again I must do battle with my kin. As his cousins were, Hakon will be banished if he survives the battle with the Norman invaders.

The army is moving at a rapid pace. There are many miles to travel. We must go to London to seal the gates against the bastard duke. Then when we have secured it, we march to the coast to rout the Norman foe.

HAROLD GODWINSON - THE LAST SAXON

WINCHESTER

It is dark inside the Cathedral. The columns reach up and beyond my seeing. The equinox is past and the days now are shorter than the nights, and dark Winter is approaching. The windows bring what little light there is but it is night, and only a half-moon shines. The shadows of bare-branched trees form on the stone-tiled floor, and as they shake in the wind, what light there is flickers like candlelight. I have woken from a deep sleep, stretched out on the floor, my body stiff and sore. I raise myself up, supporting my heavy-armoured body on my elbows. I am facing the altar, the golden cross stands tall, its Christ figure hanging in agony. I feel the pain of Our Lord. As I turn my head, I see white bones scattered across the floor; there are huge leg-bones and grinning skulls. They are a jumbled mess. Somewhere behind me were the tombstones marking the spot where the holy relics were supposed to lie: Saint Edmund, killed by The Great Army, nearly two hundred years ago; Saint Swithun, whose bones had been re-sited here and for whom the heavens had cried for forty days; Alfred, the first great Saxon King, and the greatest Wessex Man of all; Edward, his son, whose tomb was of white marble; and later, in my lifetime, the body had been interred of King Cnut, who despite all our misgivings had brought a new peace to England. He had brought the bones of his mother from Normandy to rest here and she too was up now, her bones rattling along with the rest. Yes. Cnut had brought peace, and a strengthened religion too. But this was no religious rite. The bones are up now, each in its former place, dancing around me, the eyeless heads grinning, their fleshless fingers pointing at me. They are warning me of something, and although they cannot speak, I am able to fathom their meaning. They are sending me to battle.

HAROLD GODWINSON - THE LAST SAXON

These are Saxon relics, English relics, and they command me to keep the bastard at bay. They circle round me, each time narrowing the space between me and their prancing bones. Until at last they grasp my shoulders, they shake me...

- My lord. King Harold.

I am awake now and in the gloom I see my captains standing in the doorway of my tent. One of them has roused me. It is Adulf of Tamworth.

- It is time, sir. The sun will be above the horizon soon, and the men are ready to march to Senlac.

I shake myself, wiping the sleep from my eyes, clearing the dream from my head. Winchester Cathedral has gone, along with the other spirits. We are just a few hours away from our destination. London is secure should we be unable to hold William's army back.

- Go sound the alarm. Get ready for our final march. Tell the men to be ready to fight.

Edith had been waiting for me in London with our children, and my mother, Gytha, kept her company. There are no braver Saxons. They have been in control of the city, ready to send for help if the birds bring messages. I left London and these two women, alongside Bishop Leofric, had come to bless the troops. We had halted there too long. Five days we stayed, awaiting the arrival of promised help from Mercia and Hereford. But the men never came, so I gave the order and we moved southward to the coast. Leofric, and Gytha travel westward to Hereford, while Edith returns to Walsingham.

I call the captains together and lay out the hide-skin maps. They peruse them, each man passing them around the circle in turn.

- Each of the towns is marked, and the old Roman roads that link them. These are the places William will attack if he overcomes us.

HAROLD GODWINSON - THE LAST SAXON

These are the places most at risk from the Norman invaders. They are all garrisoned, but their best protection is our victory.

The maps are back in my hand now. I show them the Portway, running from Chichester to London. If William aims to take London he will pass along this way.

- *Ermine Street, Watling Street, Ackerman Street. These old roads will take them through the country. But if we can hold them here,* and I show them on the map where Senlac lies, *then England is safe, and we can return home to our wives and mothers.*

They are weary, but they cheer and wave their fists in the air. It has been a long march; long days where we start and end in the darkness, and sleep only a few hours each night. But they are brave captains, Saxon captains, and they will inspire the men.

- *When we have tossed the Normans back into the sea we can sleep throughout the day. With Christ's help we shall be home in time to celebrate his Mass with our families. Go now, talk with your men, inspire them. Then return for a final meet before the light dawns.*

There are more cheers and beating of chests and waving of swords. As they leave, I hold onto the arm of Adulf, the bravest and boldest of all my captains. I show him an area on the map.

- *We must drive William into these marshes that surround the hill at Senlac. If we can trap him there, then our victory is certain.*

As he turns to go, I take his arm again.

- *Ensure our sentries stay awake. There must be no eavesdroppers here, nor any traitors. Ensure no-one comes near my tent tonight.*

There had been rumours that Adulf was a spy for William, but I have no evidence of anything other than his loyalty. He places his hand over his heart in a breast salute.

- By my honour and in God's name I vow to you that my body will fall, before the enemy can come to you, my King. Give me leave to make a final request. Let me be your bannerman. I shall hold your flag high above the enemy so in this way you will know my worth.

I take his sword from his sheath, and hold it above his right shoulder and Adulf kneels before me.

- You shall be henceforth the king's thegn.

I lower the sword onto his shoulder, and then allow the tip to touch the floor. He stands, salutes again, takes the sword and departs. I am alone again, and on my own I try to make sense of the dream. There are Saxon bones which must be once again laid to rest, and I am the King to do so. Perhaps I should spurn the new Abbey in Westminster and instead have my bones laid to rest alongside these great saints and kings. But that is for another time. Now we must march to battle.

This is a battle that has been coming for months. I have watched William build his fleet on his northern coast. We must hold William, stop him from reaching London. I have a plan in place to lure him to Caldbec Hill. He will see my scouts and follow them there. I shall use Adulf to lure them, with my banner, so William will think that is where my force lies. Our greatest force will be on Senlac Hill. It is there that the battle will end.

I have been betrayed! William has left the coast early and is set to thwart our plans. We arrive on the South Downs, and despite their weariness, this is a fighting force, a group of men fit and able to protect England from even a most determined enemy. We set up a shield wall, and teach them how to use a knife to hamstring an attacker, man and horse. But the Normans have taken Caldbec Hill. It is they that have seized the high ground. They are ready to defend it, and I wonder which of my earls has betrayed us. The finger is pointed at Adulf once again, but he is not alone in my suspicion. There are many in this land who will take the side of the winner and sue for more land and power with whichever man is victorious. I call my captains to gather, and tell them how we must array our forces. The standard is planted on Senlac Hill. It is of some comfort to me that I am home, and if my blood is spilt today it will be here that my body will lie. We are protected by the marshland, so we still have some advantage. But I must fight with one hand tied behind me, because I do not know who amongst my captains I can trust and which of them will betray England. There is a silence in the camp. Two armies face each other. The road to London is the prize, and it stands at our back. Behind the Normans lies the sleeve of water into which we must drive them. The final battle is close, and we seem fated to lose. As the sun slips down I remember last night's dream. There is one amongst us, a woman who has followed the soldiers in a wagon to provide food - and some comfort. She is known for her ability to read dreams and to prophesy. I send for her. I cannot sleep, and this is as good a way as any to spend the hours until dawn.

When she comes, I tell her of the things I saw, of the dancing bones in Winchester. She sits for a while in the silence that hangs over the whole camp and now smothers me here in this tent.

- *Does it have a meaning that you can read?*
- *All dreams have meaning, sire. But some are cloaked in mist and are difficult to read.*

- And this dream of ours? Is it telling us which way tomorrow will go?

- I think it does, your highness. But perhaps you would wish me to stay silent?

- Let us have your reading. We shall decide how to make use of it.

- The battle will be a bloody one, King Harold...

- We do not need your skills to tell me what I already know.

But she ignores me and continues.

- ... and England's future stands in the balance. The bones that dance are welcoming you.

- To Winchester?

- To the after-life.

- We shall all arrive there, some sooner than others.

- The dead saints will guide you to heaven.

- And the dead kings?

- They are at your side in this battle.

- Then we will win the day! Surely with Alfred and Cnut by our side, victory is certain.

I was ready to dismiss her, back to her cart.

- But there is a warning here.

- What warning?

- They appear as skeletons. It is their bones you saw, not their fleshy bodies. The kings are at your side, but they are all dead. Their bones are mixed and scattered. This is not a good omen. Perhaps the king should withdraw from the battlefield?

I want to send her away. It is as I feared. The sight of bones cavorting in the great cathedral cannot be a good sign. But before I dismiss her, she holds up her hand.

- Perhaps it is not a warning but a sign of hope. The kings who sat before you on the English throne, these great Saxons, dance in

reverence and hope, showing you that you must fight to protect their bones. They have already been mixed together. You, the rightful king, must win today and lay them properly to rest.
- You give me two readings, old woman. Which am I to believe?
- You must believe what is in your heart, King Harold. If you are to be a great king, as great as those whose bones danced before you, then your heart will guide you tomorrow.

I close my eyes and think of her words. When I open them again she has gone. And the sun has risen above Senlac Hill.

HAROLD GODWINSON - THE LAST SAXON

INVASION

WILLIAM:

God is with us. Harold has broken his oath. God and I shall punish him today. I am ready at last. I shall become King William, the first of that name that has ever ruled in England. The Norwegian King has failed, as I knew he would, but the English army is weakened. Now is my chance. My spies in the Saxon camp have served me well. News comes in every day, from intercepted pigeons. The messages are read and reattached to the birds. The bird man had come to me before we set sail. He is from Brugensis. It seems his brother, Petre, had shown the Saxons how to use birds to carry messages quickly and safely. He provides the same service for me. Who says war is a bad thing! This campaign has profited many. Two brothers getting rich, one on either side, assured of at least one successful outcome! But it is I who hope to reap the richest rewards.

England is mine, promised me by the Confessor. Harold breaks his holy vow by assuming the title of king. I know he has connived and cheated his way to the throne. Like his father before him, power is everything, and being on the right side means supporting the winner - seeing how the wind blows and setting his sails accordingly. Well, now he will pay for it. Through the early morning mist I see the king's banner: the Saxon warrior wielding his Viking axe. I look back at mine, the emblem of the Holy Roman Emperor, who has blessed our campaign. The Golden Cross shall break the head of the Saxon Warrior. I have arrived in advance of him, and he does not expect to see us assembled here.

Now is a time for patience. That is my strength. Everything I know of Harold shows me he lacks this quality. All my life I have thought before I spoke, prepared before I acted. And now when patience is most necessary, I am content to wait. The men are restless, and want to see action. They have waited so long for this day. Men who are idle, and who lack patience, are apt to be rash. So I am getting them ready. The first forays are to take place at first light. The generals, who command the crossbowmen, wait for my order. I think about the words. They must be clear.

- *Have your bowmen prepare their weapons. You are to draw their fire. Our reach is longer than theirs. Stay out of their range. They must fire their bolts at the shield wall. Make England think this is our main assault.*

The men nod. They know the plan.

- *When they loose their arrows and propel their spears we shall have their position marked. Do not engage with their army. When they start to advance, retreat, as if in disorder. Let them think they have you on the run. Let them, then, advance towards us. We shall snare them, snap them between our claws, like a crab does to its prey.*

I squeeze forefingers and thumbs together. More nods. They understand. I point them to the opening in the tent and they leave to give instructions. Harold's archers will fire at my bowmen. They will waste their arrows. They will ride into our trap. This is why I prepare. For these moments; to see a plan fulfilled. Two days ago, we passed a small farm, in a hollow, close to our encampment. There, I instructed the first section of chevaliers to wait: out of sight from the battle line; ready to attack on order. Further ahead, above Harold's lines, but hidden in the woods are the heavy horses, the destriers. There the knights carry lances and are set to charge into the rear of the attacking English if they break ranks. I know enough about this English army. They are tired, war-weary already, and they will attack as soon as they see us. Their impatience will be their weakness, Their weary moans will be their death-knell.

I watch it all unfold before me. But it is not as I planned. The English troops do not chase the bowmen. Harold holds them in check. The Saxon lines hold tight and we must use our foreign mercenaries to take the battle to them. Let them spill the English blood, and make a path for our glorious knights. The Saxons have not seen mounted warriors like these before. Once they are weakened, they will fall beneath the charging hooves.

I send for Le Blount, who is brought to me.

- *It seems Harold guesses our purpose. He holds back, when I thought he would pursue. Now we must change our plans, a little. The reinforcements from Pevensey are a day away. Harold must be made to think we do not have the stomach for a fight. His men will see us as weak and cowardly. They will break ranks, if we remain steadfast; if we remain patient.*

- *What signal will you give us when you want us to charge?*

- *A bugle, sounded three times. The men in the woods must stay hidden. When the bugle sounds, let them loose their arrows. They must fire them straight, not into the sky. From their position…*

- *… they will be like targets on a range.*

- *Like targets on a range. There will be gold for gold. For every hit they will be rewarded. The man who brings me Harold's head will be set up for life.*

- *Yes, sir. They will do as you command.*

As he leaves, I see my fingers have again assumed the crab-claw position. I will have those Saxons in a vice and I shall squeeze them until their blood runs. Until the green meadows turn red. Harold will learn what it is to break his oath.

HAROLD GODWINSON - THE LAST SAXON

HAROLD:

I sit astride my horse. I watch as the Norman bowmen retreat. I know what William plans. I sense that the men around me want to chase them, but that is what the bastard duke wants us to do.

- Hold them back, Waltheof. Hold those fyrds back. Do not let them follow. William has set a trap for us. Hold them back.

Waltheof is the son of Siward, and knows how to lead men in battle. He gives the order and the men fall back, into their lines. We have been betrayed at every turn. Our plans to be in position and repel the Norman advance are all in tatters. The Normans knew of our advance, and were here in position before us. They have the better placements now. Hidden hollows and stands of trees hide their men from us. So much of our armour was destroyed at Stamford Bridge. The Saxon men are farmers and peasants, not trained for battles such as this. The militiamen were poorly prepared. They are unprotected, especially when set alongside William's Norman troops. Our weapons are spears, axes and even stones where these have run out. Our archers are now foot-soldiers, unused to wielding weapons. The only good thing is that the Norman archers cannot restock their quivers with English arrows, and will all the sooner run out of ammunition. It is our shields that protect us from the crossbow bolts. They bounce off and leave the men unharmed.

The rising sun is reflected in the nose guards of enemy helmets, so for all the world they appear to have light shining from their eyes. But it is no more than a trick of the light, and will pass as the sun rises.

HAROLD GODWINSON - THE LAST SAXON

William is holding men in reserve, of that I am certain. But where? I can see a small wood on a hill, some way off. Perhaps they are there. There is a hollow valley behind his positions; perhaps they hide there, waiting for us to attack. William's is a well-planned campaign. I expect nothing less. My men are weary, already bloodied from their fights with the Vikings. But at least they are warriors, and know the arts of war. The new men we have gathered up on our march south are all untried.

Somehow we must hold them here, until reinforcements come from Mercia. Leofric has promised me five hundred knights, armed and ready. We must hold them until they arrive.

The sun is climbing. Whatever the outcome, it must be decided this day. Here on these fields that I call home, my fate - and the fate of all England shall be decided. Am I to continue the Saxon reign, or will the country be thrown into the darkness of Norman tyranny? The day shall decide. If they win, we have been undone by our own people, who spied and plotted against us. But all is in God's plan for us. William is still outnumbered, and we shall not move from our intent. The dream still haunts me, and I fear this may be my last day here - if God wills it then so be it. I will not die without giving good account of myself. Let battle commence. We charge their positions.

Bodies lie strewn across Caldbec Hill. The stench of their corpses is beginning to infect the air we breathe. William has sent out a small group of men to parley. One of them holds a lute and his fingers strum a tune. I know the man, remembering him from my time at

HAROLD GODWINSON - THE LAST SAXON

Caen. He is Taillefer, the duke's minstrel. And I know the tune he plays; a piece about death from The Song of Roland. I ride towards him, but he turns his horse and takes his place again among the Norman lines. Left behind is a knight who sits astride a huge beast. This is one of those heavy horses especially trained for battle. I think of more like this carving their way through Saxon bodies.

- *Are you here to parley?*

- *I am Baurain, commander of Ponthieu's forces. We met some time ago when you came to Normandy. I captured you then.*

- *Are you here to parley?*

- *William brings some music for your men, in the hope it will be a gentle sound to hear before they die.*

The man is a braggart. I demand an answer to my question.

- *Are you here to parley?*

- *I have slain many of your men today. Their heads lie separated from their bodies, decorating Caldbec Hill. Soon your head will lie sundered too, to match theirs here on this hill.*

- *This is Senlac Hill. Now you know its name, come and find me. I shall be ready for you, Baurain. And if God takes our part, it is your head that will fall.*

- *You are a liar and an oath-breaker, Harold Godwinson. And God will punish you for stealing the crown and throne that should have been our duke's. You can see our banner. You can see we bear the colours of Pope Leo. Our Holy Bishop has with him the very bones on which you swore your oath. In this way all our soldiers - and yours too - will know you are an oath-breaker and that God has abandoned you. William is the rightful king.*

Has it come to this? Has God abandoned me?

- God knows that the oath was made under duress. He will not hold me to it.

- But this army behind me shall do so, in His name.

- I ask again. Are you here to parley?

- I am here to present you with William's offer of mercy. If you will give up the crown to him here and now, then there need be no more blood shed. If you refuse, then it is a fight to the death. There will be no prisoners taken, no-one spared. But your body will be taken - dead or alive - to be spat upon. What answer shall I give? Will you return with me now so that you can make confession and England can have its rightful king take his place?

I do not answer. Instead, I ride my horse towards Baurain aiming a blow at his head. He falls from his horse.

- There is my answer, Baurain. Take that back to your king.

I watch as he rides back to the army lines. I swing my horse's head around so that I face my own men and sit before them. I draw my sword and shout out to the assembled troops.

- They ask me to give them the crown so that a Norman bastard can become your king. And this is the answer I give him. I knock his messenger to the ground. What do you say to that?

As one voice the men cried out:

- You are our King. Death to the bastard.

I raise my fist in salute.

- The enemy is coming. Raise a shield wall to keep them back. Form up as we have shown you. Do not let them pass. Lock your shields together to keep their bolts from reaching your bodies. Have courage. Stand firm. We make history today. All of England shall remember what happens here at Senlac Hill.

HAROLD GODWINSON - THE LAST SAXON

BANNERMAN

- Let the battle begin. Today whether we live or die, we shall make our mothers and fathers proud of us. If it is our blood that is spilled it will be Saxon blood for we shall never yield to Norman tyranny.

The speeches are over. I have done my best to rouse the men, to give assurances, to convince them that theirs is the true fight. It is God's will that we should defend our land. But it is now in God's hand whether we live or die; it is He who will decide if English men will become Norman vassals. But we shall give the Lord a little help - with our swords and our bows.

The Norman trumpets sound their first charge. The Norman archers fire their bolts against our shields, but we withstand them, or most of them, until our shields more resemble hedgehogs than walls. Where the bolts slip through, men lie dead. But these are brave men, Saxon men, and their courage has already been tested at York. The line does not break. The Normans have a change of plan, and now the bolts are fired higher, over the wall, and this time many more find their mark. And still the wall holds. Gradually as the sun begins its climb, it is clear that the Normans are running out of bolts and as they withdraw they shout taunts, in an attempt to draw us in.

- You are cowards. You will not fight us man to man, they shout in our own language, but with strong Norman accents. They dare us to break lines, but we hold fast. I watch from the hill top as William calls his archers back, and their place at the head of the army is taken by the foot soldiers. They approach in three waves, and I am reminded of Cnut's lesson by the sea. Unlike Cnut, we must drive this wave back; all the way back to Normandy. The central group, the largest, are led by the Pope's banner. These are William's men. To

their right I can see the flags of Flanders. To the left are the men of Brittany. They have little love for their Norman duke, but these are the bought men, mercenaries. They will have the least resolve. And though Duke William himself sits at the centre of his troops, it is not there that we shall strike first. They will fight with the greatest zeal. The first wave comes from the left, and our men withstand the onslaught. Many of us fall, but many more of the Breton army lie dead. Then it is the turn of the Flanders men. By noon, the fields are covered with corpses, and the grass is stained red from their blood.

Now it is the turn of our own shouts and taunts. William is no longer to be seen at the head of the central troops. I find a man who speaks the Norman tongue and tell him what to say.

- *The bastard is down. He is dead. You are beaten. Return home.*

And for a moment there is a lull, and I can hear the enemy seeking out their leader. Suddenly he appears. William takes the hilltop position and takes off his helmet. There he stands, the moustache, the short curly hair, and while there is blood on his face, it is not a fatal wound. Next to him is a face I know well. It is Hakon. How like his father he is. A cheer goes up, and William replaces his helmet. It seems he had been knocked from his horse, and has suffered injury. He calls out, in his accented English:

- *I see you still live, Harold Godwinson. This has been a gruelling day for both armies. You have lost half your men. Spare the lives of the other half. We give you two hours to tend your wounded, then surrender your banner to us, and we shall spare those still standing. If in two hours you still stand against us, we shall come again for you. You will all die. I have promised Hakon your head.*

I stand still, I stand silent. Then as he turns his horse I call to him.

HAROLD GODWINSON - THE LAST SAXON

- This is England, a Saxon land. There can never be a Norman king here.

William turns again and stands tall in his stirrups.

- Use the two hours well, King Harold, for it may be your last day alive. For know this: if you refuse to yield your banner to me when the two hours have passed, it will be a fight to the death and every last man standing here before us will be dead on these fields, and your head shall be cut off and held high.

The sun had passed the meridian by the time the living had dug the pits and buried the corpses. There is still time for a last rally of these brave soldiers who fight so bravely.

- They will come again to us, these Normans, and they will wield their swords and loose their arrows. But we shall withstand. England will not fall. England cannot fall, for we are Saxons, and this is a Saxon land.

The cheer that goes up moves me. I can feel the tears running down my face, but they are hidden from the men.

The truce is over. The trumpets sound and William's forces move towards us. Behind them archers let fly with more arrows, our arrows, no doubt, recovered from dead Norman bodies. Now they all come together, left, right and centre, and William sits at the centre, out of reach of our arrows but in full view of the men. This is the fourth attack of the day, and both armies are weary, but they have the advantage over us. They have not marched the length of England to be here. My men are tiring and their spirits tire too. As men fall in our lines, they are quickly replaced so that the length was maintained, but the depth grows thinner. Again and again their foot soldiers test the strength of our shields. Again and again they are driven back. William is making no progress against our brave men.

HAROLD GODWINSON - THE LAST SAXON

Then the Norman army changes its shape. The point of attack becomes a wedge, to punch a hole through our lines. In this way they will drive us back and in the space that is left their horsemen will break through swinging their swords. I turn my head to the north, but there is no help coming from there. We are betrayed by the men from London and Mercia. They wait for us to be destroyed, and then they will negotiate with William. We are alone. Men of Wessex must save England, just as they had done in Alfred's time. Our bugles and horns sound the retreat. As we make our way back to the top of the hill, a better place to make a stand, the sound of hooves comes to us. There is a dust cloud too. We are above them, on higher ground and we can see the horsemen waving flaming torches and driving frightened cattle towards our lines. But these are English cattle! Instead of running at our lines they veer off and stampede down the hill towards the valley bottom and the stream that runs through it. The horsemen see they have failed and rein in their horses but not before our archers reduce their numbers. Then the knights come at us! French and Fleming mounted soldiers charge our lines.

Our men fall like flies, swatted and crushed. The Norman chevaliers, about whom we'd heard so much, are living up to their reputations. They have destroyed the front line of troops, have driven through us and now return to hack at those who still stand.

Is this the end of us? We are being driven back down the hill. As the bodies fall, we see the next wave of attack. Giant carts are being driven at us, and then the horses are unstrapped as they are in full flight and the carts are left to run at us, like giant battering rams. They will break us. Arrows rain down on us, a deluge that pierces helmet and armour. I can see Hakon in the thick of it. My nephew wields his sword against his king.

HAROLD GODWINSON - THE LAST SAXON

Adulf has the banner. He holds it high, despite the carnage around us. He takes the reins of my horse and together we move down the hill, behind the troops, still fighting vainly. I grab the reins from him, and turn the horse back.

- *There is a battle to be fought, Adulf, a battle to be won. I must lead the men to victory.*

- *It is too late Harold. The battle is already lost. It is a matter of a few hours before all our men lie dead. William has won his battle.*

- *Then let me die with those Wessex men.*

- *No, my king. You must save yourself. Let William think he has killed you. But you will not die. With you still alive, Saxon men will have a leader in waiting. We can go to Wales. You have people there who love you for your wife's sake. They will keep you safe.*

- *I cannot do it, Adulf. I cannot run. Come. Hold the banner high above the field. Let them find me, and I will take a thousand Normans with me.*

Adulf knows it is a forlorn wish. I will not be moved. I will die in battle rather than run and hide. The blow when it comes knocks me from my horse, and despite the brightness of the day, all turns black.

I open my eyes but I can see nothing beyond the gloom. Is it night-time on the battlefield? My head aches. Am I dead, or merely dreaming? Is this the afterlife, then? The smell is of an old church; that somehow seems appropriate. Is it God's house where my body lies? Or has God forsaken me?

HAROLD GODWINSON - THE LAST SAXON

I try to stand, but I am too weary. I can see a pinprick of light which pains my eyes. It grows until it fills my head.

- *Where am I?*
- *You are at Walsingham, Harold. You are safe, here with me.*

It is Edith, and behind her I see our children.

- *How did I get here?*
- *I brought you, uncle.*

Although I cannot see him, it is Hakon's voice. I reach to my side but my sword is gone. Only an empty scabbard lies there. I try to sit.

- *Take time to rest, Harold. Hakon and I brought you here under cover of night. You are safe for now.*
- *I can never be safe in the company of a snake.*
- *Hush, my husband - for you are still my husband in my eyes. Hakon saved you. From certain death.*
- *William wanted your head, uncle.* I jar at his voice. My hands want to take him by the throat and squeeze the life from him. But I have no strength.
- *And what of Ealdgyth? Does she know of my fate?*
- *She knows only what she will have been told by William's lords - that you are dead; an arrow through your eye pierced your brain.*
- *She must know the truth.*
- *She must not, Harold. She is already across the border in Wales. She seeks to protect your son, not yet born but still in mortal danger. She will be safe with her Welsh supporters. Harold will not find her there.*

Edith puts her hand on my chest, and I feel it over my heart.

- *Hush now husband. Take time to rest. In the morning I shall come to you again.*
- *How long have I been here, Edith.*

208

HAROLD GODWINSON - THE LAST SAXON

- A week, my lord. You have been here a week.

In the morning they both return, Edith and Hakon. It is Hakon who tells me the events that followed the blow from Adulf.

The Norman foot soldiers had followed behind the carts, driving their way through the broken lines. The Saxons pushed them back, time and again, driven on by the man they thought was their king, the man who held the banner aloft. It was Adulf who led them. But the end came when the archers fired their arrows, not like rain but at head height this time, from their advanced positions. One of them struck Adulf, piercing his brain. The banner fell, and so then did the kingdom. I was sent by William to identify the body, but I was afraid to go there, as the Saxon soldiers who were still fighting would have killed me. So I was sent to fetch Edith. She was to search the fields to find your body. She was taken to where the shattered body of Adulf lay, his face unrecognisable. Edith saw that he was dressed in the king's clothes and swore it was the king who lay there, guessing at what Adulf had done. We saw the birthmark on his thigh and Edith swore it was your mark, and by that she recognised her dead husband. Edith was given permission to search the fields for her brother, whom she said had also perished at Senlac that day. We found you, Harold, unconscious, lying as though dead amongst the corpses.

Adulf's body was taken to Waltham Abbey, at Edith's request. He will be buried there with honours due to a king. My mother, Gytha, had gone to William; she had begged to have the body of her son, buried at Winchester. She offered your weight in gold in return, but William refused. Her son was an oath-breaker, he had told her, and can find no rest in God's house. But William relented and Adulf was taken to the coast to be buried in the churchyard there. I myself asked him, Harold. I reminded him that you had been a king, as well as my uncle. So it was over. For a brief moment, England had been mine. But now England has a new king, a Norman king, and I must spend my days in exile. And everyone will say that Harold, King of England was killed at the battle, and buried at Waltham. Whereas in truth Harold Godwinson lives. Perhaps I shall return one day, I shall be called; I shall return the kingdom to Saxon rule.

Acknowledgements

Thanks are due to a number of people who have helped me write this and other books.

Linda especially has been patient and tolerant despite my too-frequent frustrated cussing at IT problems encountered. The fact that this is completed owes much to her.

Friends and colleagues who form the growing band of Retford Authors Group have always shown their interest in the book's progress and share the trials and tribulations that writing brings. More about them can be found at

https://retfordauthors.wordpress.com

And finally to the writers of sagas and biographies that were constantly perused so that I could be as accurate as possible.

CONQUEST 1

HARALD HARDRADA

The Last Viking

Barry Upton

In case you missed it - the first chapter is found below.

1066

HAROLD GODWINSON - THE LAST SAXON

WE HAVE ALREADY LEFT OUR MARK; SCARBOROUGH HAS FALLEN. The treacherous mouth of the Humber welcomes us. Three hundred ships set sail from Orkney, and all but two have arrived. Their sailors survived the storm, rescued by their comrades, but their ships adorn the seabed. The sandbanks, hidden from our view, wait to wreck us and ditch us into the cold Autumn river, deceptively gilded by the early morning sun. We flow up this river of molten gold, sails lowered, oars beating a rhythmic pulse. On either bank, north and south, stand our cousins who welcome us. We had first seen them at Danes Dyke, the green scar cut into the cliffs, as we had journeyed southward along the coast. Our first thought was that this was an assault, but we saw their arms waved in salute, and knew that these were our cousins. These ships of ours are not a conquering army; we are liberators, come to free our people from the yoke of Angle tyranny. We bring them their true King. We can hear them rather than see them. Mist rising from the wide river obscures their faces. We know they are there from their rousing cheers.

On the King's ship, ahead of us, with its Raven sail, the captain reads the charts, made for us by these cousins who fish the waters and know its dangers. Without them we would surely all have perished on the sandbanks that guard the entrance as well as any harbour chains. We have lost one more ship on one such spit, but its crew and soldiers swam ashore and joined the thronging crowds. I can see the King, his head adorned with horned helmet, glinting gold from the rising sun. He stands tall and still at the prow of his ship, so that serpent and man become as one body.

The river narrows where the charts show the Humber ends and the Ouse begins, and we can see both banks more clearly. The shouts are louder: their faces are holes of sound; their arms waving welcome.

HAROLD GODWINSON - THE LAST SAXON

And we can see, too, the army forming; farmers with scythes and axes, running along the bank to keep up with us. We had been told that we would be met with warm welcome and willing men. And so it is.

Our cousins have lost their Norwegian features. Most have dark hair and sallow faces, brought about, no doubt, from the close bonding with the Angle people, native to this country, when they arrived many years before. But there is no doubting their Viking hearts.

As the sun arcs its way to lead rather than follow us, we draw alongside the northern bank. There are still many miles to go, heading northwards along the Ouse towards the great city of Jorvik. The King had forbidden them to give it the name York. This was an Anglo-Saxon name, given at the time the city was lost with the death of the great Eirik Bloodaxe. We all know the stories. They had fuelled the journey across from Norway and set us on fire and ready to fight. Jorvik will be restored to its Viking past. Then we shall march south, and all of England will fall.

The ships are tied up alongside wooden jetties, built in preparation for our landing. Food and fires greet us, as well as songs and celebrations. But I stay aboard and watch as the Viking army is welcomed as long-lost brothers: hugs with distant cousins who will soon be brothers-in-arms. King Harald himself is encircled. His name is shouted. His Raven banner is hoisted high above the moot hall, crudely erected but bearing some resemblance to those from home. He stands and speaks, this mighty king who has come to bring Danelaw to all of England. He is cheered as he calls them brothers. They have waited for this day. We are in England.

Alongside the bank two small boys play with wooden swords, as their nurse calls them to eat. They parry and prod backwards and forwards, with roars, too high pitched to be fierce, except to each other. They remind me of earlier, more innocent times. The nurse takes one by the hand and leads him inside.

1016 - 1030

I watched you, boy, at play.
I saw it in your eyes.
How you were made for greatness,
How you were made to rise.
You grew, and I could see
The man you would become.
The mighty warrior, king of all,
Whose name would span all time.

HAROLD GODWINSON - THE LAST SAXON

BOYS

Brenn Gaarder, the boy's nurse, held his hand tightly. Of course, the boy had seen the mighty King Olaf before. He was, after all, his step-brother though she was sure he was confused by this. How could his brother be this mighty king? Her mistress, Queen Ásta, went before her into the huge chamber, shepherding the boys' older siblings. His two sisters, Gunnhild and Ingrid were at the front, clinging tightly to their mother's skirts, while Guthorm and Halfdán, his older brothers, held wooden swords in their hands and tried to look brave. But she had heard them crying and fearful, as they were driven along the huge corridor that led to the Great Hall. The youngest boy brought up the rear clutching the hand of Brenn. Not that he was overawed by it all. It took a great deal to upset him, and even more to make him fearful.

This was a special day. It was a special time. King Olaf was returning home, after three years of his reign, after conquering the rebels. And his mother was eager to welcome him. The servants had laboured for weeks in preparation, and they had been sent out far and wide to gather in the best of everything. There were holes in the fields where the roots had been pulled up in their hundreds; huge carcasses had been loaded onto the carts which giant oxen pulled along the tracks leading up to the farmhouse. The boy had watched them arrive; he had asked her:

- *What does it mean, Brenn? What is it all for?*
- *King Olaf is coming. Haven't you heard?*
- *Mother said we were to be on our best behaviour. She said my brother was coming to see us.*

- Yes, your brother is coming. And there is to be a huge feast. The whole town is invited. Animals have been killed, and roots have been dug up.

Brenn could see his confusion. His brothers were Guthorm and Halfdán. Why would anyone make such a fuss over them?

- King Olaf is your mother's oldest son. He is king of the whole of Norway.

She watched him as he took it all in. Of course, the boy knew of King Olaf; he knew that he was his mother's son, but it was hard to think of him as his brother.

- Will I get to meet him?

- Tonight. At the feast in the Great Hall. All of you will meet him. Are you afraid?

- Why should I be afraid? Is he a bad man?

- No, but he is a mighty king, and he has killed so many of his enemies…

- Am I his enemy?

Brenn looked at him. She smiled and smoothed the lines on his forehead. Sometimes the boy looked older than his years. For a three-year-old he was wise and brave, not at all like his siblings, who, though older than him, were content to play on the farm and often ran back to the hall in tears after a fall, or with blood from a cut finger, where they sought out their mother for comfort. But this boy was different. He spent most of his time with her, Brenn, roaming through the woods. She remembered him one time, watching as a boar crashed through the thickets, without a whimper, without a murmur. He just stood, wide-eyed as the boar rushed past him. Brenn had been sure the boy's gaze had diverted the beast. Her heart had pounded, more afraid of the reprisals the boy's death would bring than from the tusked snarling creature. But he had stood his ground and the boar had avoided him. No, the boy was brave, there was no doubting it. He was also wayward, unwilling to do exactly as he was told.

Queen Ásta had taken her to one side.

- Stay with him, Brenn. He will be good with you. He is such a difficult boy, and the king will not tolerate his waywardness. Stay with him. Make sure he behaves. It is an important day for us. My son, has not met his siblings for some time and I want them to create a good impression.

Brenn knew what that meant. King Olaf had no heir, and there were rebels on all sides who would sell out Norway to the Danish invaders. If he were to be killed, who would succeed him? Guthorm was the next eldest but still too young and his mother would have to protect him until he was old enough to succeed. He was a royal prince, and she needed the king to accept Guthorm's claim.

- Keep him busy during the day and bring him to the Great Hall in the evening. Make sure he understands. That boy is so wilful!

Brenn had to admit he *was* wilful, but he was intelligent and curious too. In her opinion, the boy would make a much better, a much braver and a much wiser king than his older brothers. But her opinion counted for little. Brenn knew her place. She was a servant, a wet-nurse; no more than that. And she would do her best with the boy, or it would go badly for her.

Armed guards stood outside the giant doors. There were lighted torches in the recesses either side of the door and shadows danced along the walls, making Brenn shiver. But the boy's hand was steady. The two girls were close to tears, and she could tell that Guthorm and Halfdán were doing their best to be brave. Even the queen looked nervous and her hands shook. But the boy was calm. Perhaps, mused Brenn, he was too young to be afraid. The guards looked at the queen and threw back the doors. Light, heat and noise flooded the corridor and all eyes turned to them. It was Gunnhild who broke ranks first and ran straight to the king. Suddenly, the room was silent, and Brenn felt that the air had been sucked from the room. The king stood. He was tall and erect, powerful like the mighty oak, and yet all sinew and grace like the ash. The guards around him drew their swords.

- *Come, gentlemen, sheathe your weapons. There is nothing to fear here in Ringerike. We are home, and here we are loved by all. And none more so than my little sister, Gunnhild.*

He caught the girl midway through her leap towards him and swung her high above his head.

- *So little sister. Is this the way you greet your king?*

And he placed her down on the table and she knelt coyly before him. All the while, Brenn watched her mistress, heard her sharp intake of breath, and then saw her smile. The girl clapped her hands wildly and suddenly the whole room took it up. The applause was rapturous, and Gunnhild kissed King Olaf's outstretched hand. The queen knelt before her son, who moved clear of the table, swinging Gunnhild between the guards, before placing her on the floor beside her mother.

- *Welcome, my son. Welcome, my lord. Welcome, my king.*

Olaf helped her onto her feet and looked at his step-brothers, studying each in turn, as they were kneeling.

HAROLD GODWINSON - THE LAST SAXON

- So. These are my heirs?
The room fell silent. They had all heard the stories. Many had joined in the ribaldry, making fun of the king's impotence, though never in his hearing. They lived longer that way. The king had married but there was no heir. *It is a punishment from God,* he had maintained, *for marrying the illegitimate daughter of Olav.* Ásta knew otherwise. Queen Astrid, her daughter-in-law, was barren, and would never give him an heir.
- Come, mother. Let us sit together while the children enjoy the feasting.
And the noise grew again in the Great Hall. And together they sat, son and mother, King and Queen, their heads close together, and they laughed together, and the children ate greedily pulling at the cooked flesh with their teeth, ignoring the vegetable roots. Brenn sat on the other side of the boy. He ate too, but his eyes were fixed on the king. He chewed slowly. And Brenn watched him.
The daylight was fading when at last the children were sent to their beds. Brenn and the other women led them from the table. They were nearly at the giant doors when the king called to them.
- I want the boys to stay. Just for a moment. The girls may go to bed.
Queen Ásta looked up from her place beside him.
- Surely the youngest can be left to go with the girls. He is so young.
Brenn felt the boy twitch.
- I want to stay, mama. Let me stay.
Brenn tried to lead him out. The king looked into his eyes and smiled. He saw the spirit in the boy.
- Let him stay. He and I are strangers. I want to get to know him as I know his brothers. Let him stay.
Brenn bowed and waited at the door.

- Boys. Come here.

They gathered round him.

- I have a game for you. More than a game. It is a trial. Our mother is right. She nags at me, warns me that I must have an heir. Otherwise, she says, all the deaths, all the bloodshed will have been for nothing. And she is very wise, your mother, very wise. And God expects it too. So here you are, and I shall see which of you is best equipped to follow me. I have three tests for you. We shall start tomorrow at dawn. Meet me at first light on the edge of the woods, beyond the village.

Olaf waved his hand, and the brothers left the room. Guthorm and Halfdán looked for their nurse and she took their hands and led them through the dark corridors. In the torchlight she couldn't see the tears in their eyes. The boy didn't wait for Brenn. He made his way to the chamber which he shared with his brothers. Brenn caught up with him as he reached the door. They went in together. His brothers were climbing into their bed and their nurse was smoothing the blanket. Brenn took the boy's hand.

- What did he say? What did the king want?

- We are to have a trial tomorrow. The king wants to test us, a sort of game. At daybreak tomorrow.

- All of you boys?

- All. Goodnight, Brenn.

She looked at him, smiled and swept her hand through his straw-coloured hair. She knelt in front of him, their faces level. His eyes were bright and blue. His jaw was set firm.

- Goodnight, Harald. You will be a fine king.

HAROLD GODWINSON - THE LAST SAXON

The mist still hung above the valley bottom and dripped from the trees. Brenn watched the three boys as they made their way down towards the grey woods. She pulled her cloak around her in attempt to get warm. She still felt the hands of her own boy – Dag, born at dawn and named for it – whose hands had been clinging to her all night. She had unwrapped herself from his grasp, climbed from her bed and watched from the covered doorway as they descended into the wood. They stopped at a signal from one of the king's own bodyguards; they waited there, on the fringes of the wood, then one behind the other they disappeared.

Later she recalled what she had seen and heard of the trial, telling Ásta so that she might understand what had happened.

- *Guthorm led them into the wood. The King had hidden himself behind a giant oak. In front he'd laid out a net trap and both Guthorm and Halfdán walked straight into it. The King pulled them upward, the two boys hanging loosely in the net. Then the King lowered them down and as they clambered out the King simply stood and stared at them, a fierce warlike stare. Both the boys ran away shaking and in floods of tears.*

Ásta had seen the state they'd been in, even the next morning.

- *The king can be terrifying when he chooses to be. What about the boy?*

- *Harald had escaped the net, by running off just at the last moment before it was swung. He climbed a tree and waited for his brother to come and seek him out. He jumped down just as he passed, and landed on the King's back. The King shook him off, laughing at the* boy's impudence. He gave him the stare, but the boy stood his ground. The soldiers with the king were amazed by his bravery. They say he never flinched, but stood staring back at the king. King Olaf went up to the boy and pulled his hair, but young Harald never moved, never cried out. Instead, he grabbed his step-brother's moustache and tugged at it. The guards all moved forward. But the king roared with delight, lifted the boy into the air and shouted to all of them:

- See this boy. He is going to be a vindictive man when he grows up.
He turned to the guards and said:
- Beware this boy. He has all the makings of a warrior.
Then he let the boy go.
- And did he run back to the house?
- No. There was no running. He walked slowly and deliberately back up the hill. I watched him and his face beamed and his eyes glowed. Then he went back to his bed as if nothing had happened.

Ásta looked at the boy, who was playing with Dag, swinging their wooden swords high above their heads.

- And did he say nothing more, the boy?
- I asked him what had happened in the woods. And he told me everything as I have told you. Later, one of the guards saw me with him. He told me to beware of the boy. Apparently, the king had pulled the boy's face close to his and told him that he had passed the first of the trials.

That evening, as they dined together, Ásta, fearing for the safety of her boys, spoke with the King.

- You play too roughly with the boys, Olaf. You reduced them to tears. That's not a brave thing for a mighty king to do – scare his little brothers.

- *Were all of them scared, mother?*

Ásta ignored the question, telling him instead:

- *Please take greater care of them. They will be your heirs one day.*

- *Perhaps it will not come to that. Astrid...*

- *Astrid cannot give you an heir, Olaf.*

- *We shall see, mother. We shall see.*

And a smile played on his lips. There were things that his mother didn't know. Things that even a King should keep from his mother. He *would* have a son. But in the meantime, as insurance:

- *One of these boys may follow me. But which one?*

- *It should be Guthorm. He is the eldest.*

But the king had stopped listening. Ásta was angry with her oldest son. She wanted nothing more than the surety of knowing that her next-born boy would succeed Olaf and then their lives could continue. Guthorm could join Olaf in the coming years and the two younger boys would run the farms here. But Olaf was playing games. He stood up, pushed the huge carved wooden chair backwards and smiled. It was not a pleasant smile, and Ásta felt the same fear the two boys had felt.

- *It should be him who is most worthy of it. I will do my best not to frighten the boys, mother. But there will be other tests.*

It was a week later when the king visited the farmstead again. Dag and Harald were taking the runners off the sled and fitting some wheels, helped by one of the farmhands. They were going to use the cart to race against other boys in the town. Halfdán was with the cattle, helping drive them onto the higher ground now that the snow had gone. Guthorm was out with the labourers, sewing seeds for the summer corn. The king's men rounded up the three brothers and told them to meet him on the bridge. The river was swollen and ran fast beneath them. The boys sat on the wooden parapet, dangling their legs, and waited for the king to come. There was a good deal of fear in the air, as they wondered what would happen next. The king kept them waiting. Guthorm and Halfdán found some wooden offcuts dropped from the carts which had collected the felled lumber and taken it back to the village. They sat on the track together and in the mud they drew the shapes of barns and byres. Then they used the wood to build a farmyard, carving some of the bark pieces into animals. They laughed as they carved and shaped their farm.

- *What have you built here?*

It was the king. He had been watching them as they played.

- *It is the farm we shall build when we are older, King Olaf.*

- *Come, boys. Call me brother. Show me this farm.*

And he sat beside them and listened while they showed him. He smiled and nodded as they pointed out its features.

- *And where will the farmhouse be?*

Guthorm lifted up two square blocks.

- *There, brother. One each, at the heart of the farm so that we can see what the men are doing. Keep an eye on them while they work.*

The king patted both boys on the head.

- *Well done boys. Well done. Kings of the land.*

And they smiled at him, and he smiled in return. Then he went down to the river where Harald sat watching as small wooden 'boats' floated down stream, picking up the current.

- *So, boy. What game have you devised while you wait for your king?*

Harald didn't look up at him. He kept his eyes firmly on the floating wooden pieces.

- *These are my warships, King Olaf.'*
- *Perhaps, kinsman, one day you will have charge of an entire fleet of warships. Perhaps you will lead them into battle.*

News had arrived at the town. In King Olaf 's absence some of the rebels had ransacked some of the market towns, including Ribe. This was not the first attempt to snatch power and Olaf was planning his journey south, gathering an army to ride and set sail. The summer had almost passed, and before long roads and rivers would become impassable. He had to strike now. He had to assert his power, keep open the trading routes that meant so much to his people. Their last meal together was on a warm, dry evening. The doors were wide open and cloths drawn back, to get light and air into hall. He had been in Ringerike too long. He had enjoyed the days of peace and feasting. But now he must return to Nidaros where most of his army had camped. But there was something that needed to be settled, for once and for all.

Ásta entered the hall with her five children, and they sat on the bench between their mother and the king. The three boys sat closest to the him.

- *This is my last day for a while. And we have some unfinished business.*

King Olaf moved the boys so that Guthorm and Halfdán sat on either side of him.

HAROLD GODWINSON - THE LAST SAXON

- Now then boys. Your final test. I have a question for each of you. It is this: What would you most like to have?

Guthorm answered first:

-That's easy. I want ten farms with fertile lands where I could grow grain every summer. This will make us rich and important.

Ásta took Guthorm's hand in hers.

- Unless, son, you become king after your brother.

Guthorm looked at her.

- I will always strive to do my duty, mother. As king or farmer.

The King turned his attention to Halfdán.

- And what of you, brother? What would you most like to have?

Halfdán looked across at his brother.

- For me too this is an easy question my lord. I too would like ten farms, but they will be laden with cattle which will provide milk and meat to all the markets.

The king nodded.

-And what of you, young Harald? What would you most like to have?

Ásta turned to the boy, and Brenn, from her place further down the table, looked at Harald and knew what he would say. His voice was loud and clear:

- I want loyal warriors, brother.

Laughter sprang around the table. The king grabbed his hands and lifted him onto the table. Brenn watched him with pride.

- And how many loyal warriors would make you happy, boy?

Harald looked down at his brothers.

-So many that they would eat all of Halfdán's cows, with all of Guthorm's corn. In one meal.

- Look after this boy, mother. In him you have brought forth another king.

HAROLD GODWINSON - THE LAST SAXON

Ásta knew better than to argue with her son. His mind was made up. There was time to change it. But for now… the boys were young and perhaps Olaf would take another wife, who would give him a son and heir. Until then, while he was away, she would tutor Guthorm, teach him what he needed to know.

Later, watching Harald and Dag push the cart down the hill, Brenn tried to imagine the future. It had been her milk that had fed the baby boy, alongside Dag at her breast. Would this boy, her charge, be a future king? Brenn's heart glowed with pride. At the bottom of the hill the two boys dragged the cart up again, ready for the next race.

Printed in Great Britain
by Amazon

31672803R00130